SELF-LOVE WO

DON'T SETTLE FOR LESS

Subtitle: How To Love Yourself Unconditionally And Find True Happiness In The Face of Abomination

Rene Davidson

Table of Contents

PART I

Chapter 1: The Clutter in Your Life

You have probably seen many shows on television about how people hoard several different items, either because they love to shop, or they have collected many articles over time and cannot bear to part with them. It gets to the point where their closets and even their entire homes are filled up completely, and it is nearly impossible to move around. You may know people like this in your own life, or perhaps, you are one of these people. If you are reading this book, then I will assume that the clutter in your space is taking over your life.

Especially in Western society, we have a fascination with material possessions of all types. If we like something, we must have it right away. As a result, we end up purchasing so many different items, and we cannot bear to part with them, even if we don't use them anymore. After several years, our living spaces and office spaces are cluttered. This includes places like the kitchen, living room, and restrooms. So many items get collected that they end up getting stored wherever they can.

You might be wondering what the big deal is. So what if I, or anyone else, collects a lot of items? Well, the stuff is yours, and you have every right to do whatever you want with it. However, what I want to address are the psychological issues that result in clutter building up in your life, as well as the effects the same clutter has on your psyche in the long run.

Why You Have Clutter

There are numerous reasons why you have so much clutter in your life. It is not as simple as forgetting to do your Spring cleaning. Even though this could be a part of it, however, there are deeper issues as well that may reflect certain aspects of your personality. This may be more common than you think because some people are able to artfully hide their clutter behind lock doors, where you will not find it unless you dig deep. You may be hiding your own clutter so that it's not visible to you. However, when you open a certain closet, a few drawers in the house, or walk into your garage or basement, and they are filled with items that you never use, then you may have an issue with clutter.

To be fair, it's almost impossible to have no clutter at all. Having a few extra items on your desk, or a drawer with some junk in the house is not a big deal. However, if it starts to cramp your personal space, then you might have a problem. I will go over some of the main reasons why people have clutter in their homes. See which ones you can relate to.

You Don't Recognize What Clutter Is

Many people allow clutter to build up in their homes because they don't recognize what it is. They have a hard time deciphering between what is valuable and what is just taking up space. Some items were once valuable but haven't been used for a long time. Because it can be hard to recognize what clutter is, people have a hard time letting anything go. They will look at something, suspect that it could come in handy down the line, and then never get rid of it.

You Don't Know How Long You Should Keep Something

This is a huge area of confusion in almost any household. How are you supposed to tell how long to keep something? Many people have no concept of when and where to let things go. I am not just talking about tools or appliances here. This can be related to anything. For example, people still have birthday or holiday cards that are decades old. It is nice to look at these cards and conjure up some nice old memories, but how many reminders of the past do you actually need?

You Don't Know How to Store Things

People often do not know how to store things. It might be because they forget, or they do not know where it should go. Suddenly, you will find something hidden in the weirdest section of your house, or worse, not be able to find it when you need it.

Along the same lines, you have no good organizing routine. Perhaps you are not an organized person, in general. This is not an indictment on you personally. Many individuals lack the ability to organize everything in their lives, and this grows worse with the more items they obtain. You can actually declutter for about

15-20 minutes a day for several days straight, and many of your items will disappear.

You Are Not Using Clutter Busters

Clutter busters are items, such as trays, baskets, jars, hooks, or folders, that can be used to place your materials in specialized locations. Yes, you will still have the items in your home, but at least they won't be in your way all the time. Can you imagine having a toilet brush on your coffee table? I certainly hope not.

Buying Too Many Things, You Don't Need

This is probably the most obvious one. How many of us don't buy things we don't need? From aspirational shopping to impulse buying, our homes are filled with things we bought on a whim. Aspirational shopping comes from our interest in actually doing something, only to realize it's not for us. However, we don't take the time to get rid of the items afterward. For example, we might watch a musician playing the guitar and want to be like him. So, we buy a guitar, end up hating it, or get to busy to practice, and then put it in a closet somewhere.

If you genuinely have an interest in learning something, I think it's great. But at least stick to it for a little while to give it a chance. If you end up not liking it, then sell the items or donate them to someone who will use them.

In this last instance, you may know you are a clutter bug, and may not want to be one, but you can't seem to let things go. You have a weird attachment to them and might not know why. This will require a deeper understanding of who you are and why particular items are hard to let go, even if you never use them.

Assess your own situation and determine which of these reasons are causing you to hold onto clutter. It might be a combination of things, which is fine. The important thing is to recognize why the spaces in your life seem so busy when they do not have to be.

Endowment Effect

There is a phenomenon known as the endowment effect, which can also explain why people have a hard time getting rid of things. This is a type of bias that occurs when people overvalue something simply because they own it. It might have been given to them, or they bought it years ago, but would never consider getting it now. However, since they own it, they place a greater worth on it.

This psychological bias has resulted in many people not being able to part with something. They are not even willing to sell it at a fair price, because they feel no one will pay the real value of it. The ironic part is the person with the attachment would never consider buying the article for nearly the same price they are trying to sell it for. For example, if they have a special coffee mug, they will put it on the market for $10, but if they saw the mug in a store, they will not even consider purchasing it. It seems that ownership gives people a certain sense of power, and they hate giving it up.

There is also a concept in psychology known as loss aversion. This is where people feel the pain of losing something at a higher intensity than the joy of gaining something of equal value. For example, if a person loses five dollars, but then finds five dollars somewhere else, the original pain of losing money will still affect them more than the joy of finding money. This can be another reason the endowment effect is so powerful. If a person owns an item, getting rid of it in exchange for the actual value will not be acceptable to them. Therefore, individuals who are impacted by this mindset will overly price something to compensate for their feelings of loss.

The endowment effect is an interesting bias that is still being studied today. It is not completely understood why this mindset affects people. But it definitely does.

The Consequences of Too Much Clutter

While you may think that too much clutter just means you will have a hard time moving around stuff, the consequences actually go much deeper than that. There are numerous negative results that happen due to excess clutter, and some of them might surprise you. After this, you will probably be more motivated to clean up a little bit.

Your Stress Levels Increase

People who live in cluttered environments have higher levels of stress and fatigue. Even increased amounts of the stress hormone, cortisol, was found in their blood. Because individuals stayed in these environments, their cortisol levels never dropped throughout the day, causing chronic stress, more chronic disease risks, and even greater mortality risk.

Your Diet Is Impacted in A Negative Way

Psychological studies have also shown that people who live in more orderly environments tend to choose healthier snack options that those in cluttered areas. Since stress leads to unhealthy snacking, being around too much clutter will lead to poor dietary habits. People also tend to overeat with too much stress.

You Can Develop More Respiratory Issues

Homes that are cluttered tend to attract more dust because there are extra physical items it can settle on top of. Extra dust in the air can eventually lead to respiratory issues in the long run, and can also exacerbate active problems, like asthma or COPD.

The more items you have inside your home, the more dust is generated. This will also attract dust mites. Furthermore, if your clutter gets way too excessive, then several areas of your home will become exceedingly difficult to reach and clean. As a result, more dust will build up. Of course, respiratory issues can lead to even more health consequences.

Your Safety Is Threatened

Too much clutter can lead to an unsafe environment where people can trip and fall easily. You also have more items to bump into when you can't see. In addition, it can be difficult to move around, and essential exits might be blocked. This causes a huge risk if you ever have to evacuate your home urgently. A fire can also spread much more quickly if you have a lot of combustible items lying around.

Your Love Life Is Jeopardized

Clutter can negatively affect marriages, too, as people who have difficulty parting with things may build resentment in their spouse. The clutter does not just impact you, but everyone else in your home too. If the person you love is bothered by the clutter and you're not, then your marriage can definitely suffer.

If you are not married and just dating, imagine what your date would think if she saw your home, and it is completely disorganized. If they don't run for the hills right away, they might do so as soon as the date is over.

Your Kids Will Be Upset

Yes, your kids, who you constantly tell to clean their room, will be upset with excess clutter. Studies have found that kids who live in a cluttered environment tend to have more distress, which will affect other areas of their lives.

You Will Become Isolated

A large number of adults say they won't invite anyone over to their house if they feel it is too messy. If you have a lot of clutter and you feel this way, then you likely have not had many guests in your house recently. This can cause you to become isolated from the world, especially if you are a homebody. If you like to spend all of your time outside of your home, then I guess this one won't be too relevant for you.

A person who lives in clutter rarely confines these tendencies to their home life. They will carry them everywhere, including their work environment, as you will see with some of the following examples.

You Will Miss Out On Getting Promoted

Untidiness at work, including a messy desk, a chaotic briefcase, or an unorganized filing system, can have negative impacts on your job performance. You will likely spend too much time looking for things and not enough time actually doing any work. Your boss will notice your clutter as well, and this can put you in a bad light when it's time to hand out promotions. According to a study on the career website, CareerBuilder, roughly 28% of employers are less likely to promote someone who keeps their workspace messy. They feel that disorganization leads to poor job performance, and they are right to think this way.

You Are More Likely to Miss Work

The National Institute of Mental Health studies have found that individuals in a cluttered environment are more likely to miss work. They estimated an average of seven missed days per month, which is an excessive number.

Your Productivity Decreases

While you are in a cluttered environment, your ability to focus is severely impeded. If you have many different items within your visual field simultaneously, they all compete for your brain's attention. You cannot give it equally to all of them, so you focus more on things that you are interested in. More often than not, that usually not your work projects. If you have papers, pens, food, and various other things on your desk, you will have a hard time getting any work done at all, and your productivity will be greatly affected. Once again, the bosses will take notice, and you won't be in very high standing when they hand out raises or promotions. In fact, they may not keep you at all if you're not performing as you should.

See how many negative results can happen to your career by keeping your workspace too cluttered? It will behoove you and your career aspirations to change this quickly.

You Will Develop Poor Spending Habits

When you live in a cluttered environment, it can become difficult to find things. As a result, you will buy another item of the same kind, not realizing it was hiding under all of your rubbish.

You Can Go into Debt

This last one may not be relevant anymore due to the ability to make online payments, but those of you who rely on paper bills as a reminder to pay them will suffer greatly. Bills become lost and forgotten, resulting in extra fees. If these are really important bills like credit cards or house payments, then additional problems will occur with the banks and financial institutions. Even your credit score will start to decline.

As you can see, the various negative effects of too much clutter can impact every area of your life. It can significantly decrease your physical and mental health and create many psychological issues for you. With the impact on career and relationships too, you will fall further down into the abyss.

Think about your own life and determine how much of an effect clutter has on your mindset. I am willing to bet that you feel much better sitting in a particular area after you have cleaned it up a little bit. Now that we have established some reasons why people collect clutter and the negative consequences associated with it, I will go over some action steps to get rid of clutter in your life.

Clutter is Not Just Physical

I have spoken a lot about the physical clutter around your home or office. All of this is very distracting and can cause you to lose focus. Too many stimuli will compete for your focus, and you will not be able to give any of them your full attention. Important issues will go right over your head.

Physical clutter is bad, but it is not the only kind you have to contend with. Clutter also includes technology, which is a growing problem in this day and age. We get emails all the time from many different sources. Sometimes we don't even know who the email is from, and just ignore it. However, we often don't erase the email or unsubscribe from the individual, which results in even more unnecessary items in our inbox. Junk email is literally regular junk mail on steroids. When we get so many different ones from various sources, it clutters our files, and we become extremely overwhelmed, just like with physical clutter. As a result, a lot of important information falls through the cracks.

With so much information coming in, it becomes very distracting, and our ability to focus and remain productive decreases. Once we become overwhelmed, we no longer answer emails; we simply scroll through them and hope we did not miss anything important. Suddenly, an important email from our boss comes through, and we never catch it. As a result, critical information was missed, which can jeopardize your company and even your job.

Digital clutter is not exclusive to too many emails. Having an excessive number of programs or apps on your computer, carrying around multiple devices, managing multiple social media accounts, and storing a lot of photos can also be overwhelming in the same manner. In many cases, once a person's data gets used up, they just buy more space, rather than clearing out what they have. It's usually quicker and easier that way. It may not seem like a big deal in the present moment, but after a few months or years, you will realize just how much your productivity and focus has decreased. Increasing productivity and getting things done will be a major topic of this book.

Chapter 2: Breaking Your Relationship With "Stuff"

Now that we have established the psychological reasons people hold onto things, it is to incorporate strategies that will help you get rid of excess clutter. While decluttering can be very difficult at first, it can also be very freeing and have a positive impact on your life in every way. In this chapter, I will go over various different techniques for you to start reducing your personal items or reorganizing them in a proper fashion. Either way, your home, and workspace will become more appealing and habitable.

Getting Over the Endowment Effect

Since the Endowment effect has such a great impact on your ability to get rid of things, I will go over some tips to help you overcome it. Once you go through these steps, you will realize how little value the items in your life actually have and how ridiculous it was to hold onto them for so long when you weren't using them.

The following are a few simple ways to get over the endowment effect:

- Well, now that you know what the endowment effect is, you can become aware that it is personally affecting your life. If you are having difficulty letting go of something you don't need, tell yourself it's the endowment effect and break the curse.

- Using your imagination can help here too. If you are having a hard time getting rid of something, imagine that you do not own it anymore. This can help weaken the emotional ties you have to it.

- Take the items you no longer use and put them in a sealed box. Now, put them somewhere like an attic or basement. Give yourself a timeline, like three months or six months, and if you do not open that box, then give it away without unsealing it.

- Write down your "why." Why is it important for you to declutter, and what value will it bring to your life?

These tips will help you overcome the power that the endowment effect holds on you, and it should become a little easier to declutter your life after this.

More Decluttering Tips

In this section, I will go over some more decluttering tips to help you reorganize your life. You can use one, or all of these, to start getting rid of unnecessary items. Through some of these steps, you can also determine which items you still need and the ones you can get rid of without a thought.

- Make the process less overwhelming if you are new. Start with five minutes a day and use this time to declutter what you can. From here, raise the time at your comfort level.

- Give one item away each day. By the end of week one, you will have given away seven items. By the end of the year, you will have given away 365. You will definitely see your belongings disappearing quickly. If you want to make the process faster, you can certainly increase the amount you give away.

- Get a large trash bag and fill it up with as many items as you can. After filling it up, tie the bag and donate to Goodwill or another donation service before you change your mind.

- Take all of your clothes and hang them facing backward. Whenever you wear an item, hang them back up facing forward. After several months, the clothes that are still facing backward should be donated.

- Use the 12-12-12 rule for getting rid of items. Take out 12 things that you plan on donating, 12 things that you plan to throw away, and 12 things that you will keep for now. This will lessen the impact of getting rid of things because you can see what you're still keeping.

- Go into your home with a first-time visitor mindset. Look around the house and determine how you would clean and reorganize the place, including what items you would get rid of. This is a mind trick you can use to detach yourself from the things inside.

- Choose a small area of your home and take before and after pictures. For example, take a small section on your kitchen counter that has clutter, snap a quick photo, and then clean off the area. Take another photo right after that. Having this visual will help you keep that area clear. Start doing this with other areas of your home too.

Decide whichever tip works best for you and then go from there. If there are others that you come up with, that is fine too. The goal is to declutter in whatever way necessary, so get creative in your approach.

Stop Buying Stuff You Don't Need

If you are decluttering the stuff out of your personal space, but also buying things you don't need at the same time, then it defeats the purpose. You are just replacing one set of items for another. As a result, decluttering will mean nothing as your environment will just become busy again. The goal of decluttering is to keep your space from becoming overfilled. This requires a combination of getting rid of stuff and not buying new stuff. The following are some effective ways to stop buying unnecessary items.

Keep Away from Temptations

If you have a tendency to splurge on things you don't need, then don't tempt yourself by window shopping or going into a store to look around. You might also want to stop getting shopping magazines and cancel online subscriptions to stores. You may not be thinking about buying an item until you see it, and then suddenly, it is in your room just sitting there.

If you must go to the store, make a list and stay laser-focused on it. If you know where the items are, then only go to those sections of the store. You can also shop online and have the items delivered, so you don't actually go out.

Avoid Retail Seduction

Retail stores are masterful at seduction, from hiring the best salespeople, to proper lighting, placement, and layout. All of this is done to draw in their customers, and many people fall for it. This is why someone ends up spending 20 dollars on a coaster set when a five-dollar one would have worked.

Avoid retail seduction by being aware of it. When you see an enticing item, mentally isolate it from its environment and see if the appeal is still there. Also, imagine it being placed in a bin at the thrift store and see if you still want to buy it.

Take Inventory

Oftentimes, we buy things because we don't have enough. However, if you take regular inventory of everything in your home, including inside the drawers, you will find more than you realized. The desire to buy more will go down. Even after you declutter, you will still have many items.

Practice Gratitude

Be mindful of the things you have in your life, both tangible and intangible, and show gratitude for them. Again, you will realize your life is more fulfilling than it appeared beforehand.

These are just a few tips to keep you from going on a shopping splurge and refilling your house with items that are useless. Once you see the powerful effects that decluttering will have on you, it will be lifechanging in so many ways. This is why so many people who became minimalists are much happier now.

Calculate Cost Vs. Labor

The trick here is to figure out how much something costs, and then determine how many hours you would have to work to make up that money. This can really be eye-opening for you. Determine if the labor hours are worth the item you want to purchase.

Keep Your Big Picture in Front of You

When you are spending money day-to-day, it can be easy to lose track of things. You may not realize how much one day of spending can take you away from your ultimate goals. This is why it's important to keep the big picture at the forefront of your mind. Use whatever reminders you need to accomplish this.

A lot of the techniques I have gone over about tricking your mind or shifting the mindset away from what you are used to. Incorporating all of these strategies into your life on a regular basis will give you the best results.

The Benefits Of Decluttering

The benefits of decluttering are another thing you can keep in mind to help you stay focused on eliminating excessive items from your life. The process really is freeing once you give it a chance. The following are a summary of some of the benefits of decluttering. I will get into many more over the next few sections.

- Reduced stress and anxiety related to all of the clutter.
- Reduced number of allergens, like dust, pet hair, and pollen that can accumulate on surfaces.
- A cleaner and more sanitary environment.
- Save extra money and even make money by selling things.
- Extra space in your home for fun activities.
- Less shame in inviting guests.
- Your home will be safer to move around in. There will be fewer things to run into.
- Family or others who are living with you will appreciate it.
- You will realize how many things you can actually do without.

Decluttering Equals Increased Focus and Productivity

Imagine a housecat for a moment. They easily become distracted by shiny lights, new toys, or any hanging objects. If you put something in front of a cat's face, they will be mesmerized by it. If you place multiple items in front of them, they will not be able to figure out which one to focus on. Our minds can become the same way if we let them.

Lucky for us, our brains have a natural filtering mechanism that allows it to not be distracted by every little thing around is. So, when you are performing a task, you may not notice the slight wind outside, the cars driving by on the front seat, or every single person that walks by. Our brains do a great job of shutting out what we don't need to see, hear, or feel every moment.

The problem here is, it takes a lot of energy to filter things out, and this energy is finite. This means that the more things around us that have the potential to catch our attention, the more energy the brain uses, and the more quickly it will dissipate. Therefore, the more clutter you have, the quicker your brain will lose its ability to focus, and you will become distracted more easily.

It is simple to see, then, that decluttering will increase your focus because you have fewer things that will drain the energy required to keep it. Try something as soon as you can. While you are sitting at your table, remove a few items from it and see how many less distractions you have. Remove any objects that are unnecessary to the task at hand. Many people will keep snacks at their desks. Avoid doing this because then you will just be snacking constantly, instead of working. When you're hungry, actually get up, and make yourself something. Put in the work.

Notice how much clearer your mind feels after doing this. When our surroundings become too busy, so does our mind. While some people believe that a busy mind creates productivity, it is quite the opposite. A clear mind with focus is what allows true productivity, so if you want to get things done, clear up your environment, and clear up your brain.

Decluttering and Improved Health

Decluttering will improve many aspects of your health. Notice some of the healthiest people around you, and you will see that their living or workspaces are immaculate compared to others. I will go over a few ways that decluttering will have positive health consequences.

Improved Healthy Habits

When you declutter your home, you will develop healthy habits. The main reason for this is that certain items will be easier to get to and will more likely get used. For example, if you open your closet and quickly find the vacuum or broom, you are more likely to use them. If your vacuum is behind a wall of various items, you will not want to put in the effort to get it. This goes for cooking, as well. If your kitchen is filled up with supplies, like extra appliances, cookware, dirty dishes, and various articles that don't need to be there, you are less likely to cook meals at home. There is a greater chance that you'll just cook a microwave dish or buy fast food.

Better Self-Care

When living in a clean and sanitary environment, you will have better self-care overall. It will be easier and more appealing to exercise in an open space. Also, your sleeping habits will improve because it is easier to be restful in less busy surroundings. Finally, people who declutter slowly develop the habit of remaining clean, which improves hygienic practices.

Losing Weight

This may seem like an odd connection, but it's true. People are much more likely to be overweight if they live in a cluttered environment. A study done by the University of Florida estimates about a 77 percent higher chance of being overweight or obese. This is related to the busy lifestyles that people have, which is common with people who do not declutter. When you learn to declutter, you also learn to slow down. You also become much more organized. This gives you more time to eat properly and exercise.

Too much clutter in your home can impact your ability to relax and enjoy yourself. The immense amount of distractions will ever allow your mind to stop getting distracted. It will be hard to immerse yourself in a relaxing activity, like reading, watching a movie, or taking a bath. You will just feel cramped, and trying to calm your nerves will be an uphill batter you cannot win.

All of these benefits will work in conjunction to improve your physical and mental health.

Having More Space

It is easy to see that decluttering opens up space around you. Not only will you have a greater physical area to work in, but a larger mental space to think. You will become more creative because it will be easier for you to open up your mind. This is where some of your best ideas will come into play.

Having an open space can increase your confidence and self-efficacy. A lot of this has to deal with the decluttering process. As you remove items from your life or reorganize them, you will have to make some important decisions. Getting rid of stuff is not easy, and you will have to think quite a bit. This will improve your capability to come up with solutions, which will definitely make you more confident in yourself. This will also give you more energy because you put yourself in the mode of getting things done. This relates back to productivity.

Having more open space reduces family and relationship tension. An excessive mess can lead to major arguments. Disagreements may arise over who causes the clutters, and therefore, who should get rid of it. Parents will often become frustrated with their children because it will take forever to find something. Do not underestimate how beneficial having more open space can be for your personal relationships.

Think back to when you moved into your home or office. This was prior to moving in any furniture or personal items. Even if it's a small space, it certainly looked much bigger than it appeared before adding extra items. Now, imagine how much bigger your space will become from just removing half of your stuff out. You will truly appreciate the extra space when you have it.

6-Week Decluttering Challenge

You can certainly take as long as you need to declutter your home, office, car, or other space that you occupy regularly, but using a challenge can light a fire under and hold you accountable for making some real changes. You can also bring in the help of a friend to help hold you accountable. Let them know what you plan to accomplish each week, and then bring them in at the end of every week to assess your progress. Take before and after photos, too, so you can have your own visuals.

It is a simple process. Starting from the beginning, pick a certain part of your home that you will focus on each week. For example, week one will be dedicated to the kitchen and dining room. Then, the second week will be dedicated to the living room. The third week will be dedicated to one or two bedrooms, depending on the amount of clutter. In the fourth week, the focus will be on the garage. In the fifth week, you can start on the basement. Finally, the sixth week can be used for any leftover closets or the laundry room. This is just an example, and you can make up your own plan based on your particular spaces. You can break down each week into smaller goals, as well.

Here is a visual:

- Week 1: Kitchen and dining room
    - Declutter the countertops-Day 1
    - Declutter the fridge-Day 2
    - Declutter the cabinets-Day 3
    - Declutter the pantry-Day 4
    - Declutter the stove and oven-Day 5
    - Declutter the dining room table-Day6
    - Declutter any other tables or cabinets in the dining room-Day 7

It may be best to start in the kitchen because it is a high traffic area in the house. From here, you can cover the other areas of your home and break it down day by day. It is really that simple. You just have to maintain discipline. Feel free to incorporate any of the strategies for decluttering I went over earlier.

After doing the six-week challenge, give yourself a pat on the back for your accomplishment. You can even reward yourself. In fact, you can also give yourself small rewards at the end of each week, granted that you accomplished what you needed to. If you stick to the challenge, you will not believe how much more space you will have. Your home may even look bigger than before.

Now that we have established the benefits of decluttering and how you can get this done in your life, the rest of the book will cover how to move forward and start getting things done in your life.

∧

PART II

Chapter 1- What is Self Compassion

What is the self-compassion? Have you thought about it or experienced it from someone?

The truth is, having compassion for yourself is not different from having compassion for other people or animals. Having self-compassion is being kind to yourself and understanding to your needs when you face personal failures. Think about how you would talk and console a friend who's going through a rough time- what would you say to them? Would you be harsh to them? Would you say things that bring them down even more?

The answers to those questions are of course a big NO. You would do what all good friends do- bring them up when they feel down, hug them and tell them everything is going to be ok, telling them that you'll be there for them to talk to or if they need help. Self-compassion is acting this same way towards yourself when you go through a rough patch. You notice the suffering and you empathize with yourself by comforting yourself, offering kindness and understanding.

Kristin D. Neff and Katie A. Dahm are two prominent are two names synonymous with the research on self-compassion. In their book, the Handbook of Mindfulness and Self-Regulation, it states that there are three primary components to self-compassion:

1. Self-kindness

2. Common humanity

3. Mindfulness

To understand self compassion, we need to consider what it means to feel compassion on a general level. Here are some views of compassion:

The Buddhist point of view of compassion is given to our own as well as to others suffering.

Goetz, Keltner & Simon- Thomans, 2010: Compassion is the sensitivity to the suffering that is happening, coupled with a deep desire to alleviate that suffering

Neff, 2003a: Self-compassion is compassion directed inwards, referring to ourselves as the object of concern and care when we are faced with an experience of suffering

The Three Elements of Self-Compassion

The key to understanding self-compassion is to understand the difference between this trait and more negative ones. Sometimes when we give ourselves self-compassion, it may be construed as narcissism to a point, which is why it is important to know what is self-compassion and to what degree is it considered self-compassion and when it isn't.

1. *Self-kindness is not Self-Judgement*

Self-compassion is being understanding and warm to ourselves when we fail, or when we suffer or at moments when we feel inadequate. We should not be ignoring these emotions or criticizing yourself. People who have self-compassion understand that being human comes with its own imperfections and failing is part of the human experience. It is inevitable that there will be no failure when we attempt something because failure is part of learning and progress. We will look into how failure is a friend in disguise in the next chapters. Having self-compassion is also being gentle with yourself when faced with painful experiences rather than getting angry at everything and anything that falls short of your goals and ideals.

Things cannot be exactly the way it should be or supposed to be or how we dream it to be. There will be changes and when we accept this with kindness and sympathy and understanding, we experience greater emotional equanimity.

2. *Common humanity and not Isolation*

It is a common human emotion to feel frustrated especially when things do not go the way we envision them to be. When this happens, frustration is usually accompanied by irrational isolation, making us feel and think that we are the only person on earth going through this or making dumb mistakes like this. News flash- all humans suffer, all of us go through different kinds of suffering at varying degrees. Self- compassion involves recognizing that we all suffer and all of us have personal inadequacies. It does not happen to 'Me' or 'I' alone.

3. *Mindfulness is not Over-Identification*

Self-compassion needs us to be balanced with our approach so that our negative emotions are neither exaggerated or suppressed. This balance act comes out from the process of relating our personal experiences with that of the suffering of others. This puts the situation we are going through into a larger perspective.

We need to keep mindful awareness so that we can observe our own negative thoughts and emotions with clarity and openness. Having a mindful approach is non-judgemental and it is a state of mindful reception that enables us to observe our feelings and thoughts without denying them or suppressing them. There is no way that we can ignore our pain and feel compassion at the same time. By having mindfulness, we also prevent over-identification of our thoughts and feelings.

Discovering Self Compassion

You're so dumb! You don't belong here loser! Those jeans make you look like a fat cow! You can't sit with us! It's safe to say we've all heard some kind rude, unwanted comments either directly or indirectly aimed at us. Would you talk like this to a friend? Again, the answer is a big NO.

Believe it or not, it is a lot easier and natural for us to be kind and nice to people than to be mean and rude to them whether it is a stranger or someone we care about in our lives. When someone we care is hurt or is going through a rough time, we console them and say it is ok to fail. We support them when they feel bad about themselves and we comfort them to make them feel better or just to give a shoulder to cry on.

We are all good at being understanding and compassionate and kind to others. How often do we offer this same kindness and compassion to ourselves? Research on self-compassion shows that those who are compassionate are less likely to be anxious, depressed or stressed and more resilient, happy and optimistic. In other words, they have better mental health.

Conclusion

It does make sense that people who have better self-compassion are happier and optimistic about their future. When we continuously criticise ourselves and berate ourselves, we end up feeling incompetent, worthless and insecure. This cycle of negativity continue to self-sabotage us and sometimes, we end up self harming ourselves.

But when our positive inner voice triumphs and plays the role of the supportive friend, we create a sense of safety and we accept ourselves enough to see a better and clear vision. We then work towards making the required changes for us to be healthier and happier. But if we do not do this, we are working ourselves towards a downward spiral or chaos, unhappiness and stress.

In the next chapters, we will look into the benefits of self-compassion, self-esteem, how to get rid of negative self-talk, mastering our emotions as well as practical exercises towards becoming self-compassionate.

Chapter 2- Benefits of Self-Compassion

You've probably heard your parents say time and time again to treat others as you would want them to treat you. Therefore, we are often taught to be empathetic and compassionate to others who are facing difficulties and challenges in their life. However, when faced with our own personnel challenges be it in our everyday lives, work and relationships, we often find ourselves becoming our own worst enemy. Hence we become too critical and judgmental on our own selves and in turn prevent any healing process from taking place.

Therefore, instead of being self-critical to oneself, we need to develop the concept of self-compassion in combating our negative thoughts and self-criticism that keeps us from overcoming our obstacles and challenges.

Self-compassion is defined as being compassionate to our own suffering, inadequacies, weakness and failures. As we know from the previous chapter, Kristin Neff, an associate professor at department of educational psychology in the University of Texas further breaks down self-compassion to 3 key elements which are self-kindness, common humanity and mindfulness.

Self-kindness is about recognizing our flaws and issues as well as being caring to oneself when going through bouts of hardship and challenges. Common humanity on the other hand, puts emphasis that the suffering and anguish we go through is all a natural part of being human and it's a normal part of everyday life. Lastly, mindfulness deals with the individual's ability to take a middle path in addressing their sufferings so as not to neglect or overthinking the situation.

Various research done on the topic of self-compassion indicates that individuals who practice self-compassion have a far greater psychological health than those who lack it. The individuals who practice self-compassion have a more positive life satisfaction, happiness and optimism. Apart from that self-compassion is also connected low levels of anxiety, self-criticism and depression. As such, in a way self-compassion can be used as a tool to develop inner strength when facing challenges in every aspect of our life.

So we know what self-compassion is and sure it helps us lead a better life and have better relationships. What other aspects of self-compassion are there? Here are some major benefits you can reap from being self-compassion. We explore it in terms of work, relationships and in life.

Self-Compassion At Work

Our daily work environment can be a long-lasting love-hate relationship with its own ups and downs that one has to face on a daily basis. As such, we are constantly bombarded with undue stress in meeting deadlines, reports and customer expectations. Many at times, we will face moments that completely overwhelm us and have a negative impact on us. This can be caused by numerous factors such as a negative remark by a colleague, superior or even a customer, failure to reach sales targets or goals, not getting that raise or promotion that you so deserve or even by making an unintentional mistake at the job. Since we all strive to achieve more and be perfect at our jobs, this negative circumstances will have an adverse effect if not dealt properly and swiftly.

Self-compassion can be used at work through the following means to reap various benefits: -

- Conducting a post-mortem to review the shortcomings and failures of a certain project or task and learning from these failures to prevent similar occurrences in the future.

- When facing criticism and rejection from colleagues, superiors and customers, instead of being self-critical and falling into complete despair, we will be able to be calm and focus our energies and thoughts of improving ourselves and not to allow stress to overwhelm ourselves.

- Applying self-compassion at work also helps us in being resilient through difficult scenarios especially is situations that we don't get a certain reward or promotion that we think we deserve.

- Self-compassion enables us to be more creative. When we fail a project or we do not complete a task or when a work event doesn't go as expected, being self-compassionate to ourselves will help us to look back at the series of events and instead of berating ourselves, we look back and see what we could have done better and learn from our mistakes. It makes us becoming more creative the next time around.

- Self-compassion builds trust. It enables you to be transparent and authentic, makes it easier for people to connect with you because you are your true self.

- Showing genuine compassion to yourself also means showing compassion to the people around you. When you show compassion to yourself, you extend this feeling to your co-workers and it makes them feel safe.

- Self compassion allows you to allow yourself and your team implicit permission to do their very best without worry of punishment or repercussions if something doesn't go right.

Self-Compassion In Relationships

In the topic of relationships be it a romantic or non-romantic relationship, we often find ourselves in situations of disagreement from time to time. And these can sometimes lead to moments of stress and unhappiness between oneself and their significant other/parent/sibling/friend. Self-compassion provides various ways much like our situations at work to help us deal with this issues and challenges. Many studies done on this matter point that self-compassion when used have the following positive impact on relationships: -

- Individuals who practice self-compassion know that every individual as well as themselves aren't perfect and are subjected to weaknesses and shortcomings
- They are able relate to their partners much better
- They are more warm and compassionate in understanding a situation
- They are more open to compromising to resolve a situation
- Individuals who are self-compassionate have better empathy. The bring out the best in their partners.
- They are more responsive and aware to the issues that their partner faces
- They are better listeners, they listen to understand and not answer
- People who practice self-compassion own up to their mistakes

Studies also have shown that individuals that lack self-compassion tend to have a negative effect on people around them which may lead to isolation. As such, those people who practice self-compassion have healthier and happier relationships and have a bigger a wide social circle.

Self-Compassion In Life

When encountering difficulties in daily life which can range from a number of issues/aspects such as health to financial issues, we need to act by being compassionate and kind to ourselves. When faced with various issues on a daily basis, self-compassion allows us to look for solutions to take care of oneself instead of berating or being overly critical of one's lack of accomplishments or weaknesses.

With that being said, an individual who practices self-compassion will look into various ways to engage their mind and body into healthy activities that can stimulate them and lets them focus on positive aspects instead of groveling on a negative situation. This can be in a form of an exercise, a hobby, prayer or even a warm bath or a cup of tea to calm themselves down.

Self-compassionate individuals tend to be more: -

- Happier
- Satisfied with life
- Resilient
- Emotionally intelligent
- Have better coping mechanisms
- Optimistic
- Creative
- Less judgemental
- Better goal-getters
- It greatly reduces mental problems

As such, cultivating the habits of self-compassion in every aspect of our life will allow to become the best version of ourselves and allow us to live much happier with the right mindset.

Chapter 3: Myths about Self Compassion

Many people do not have any issues with showing compassion to other people-it is a commendable quality. Compassion is often seen with kindness, tenderness, understanding, sympathy, empathy and of course the impulse to help those in need, whether human or animal.

However, with self-compassion, that is a different story altogether. For plenty of people, having self-compassion often relates to negative qualities such as self-serving, self-pity, self-centered, indulgent and just selfish. We seem to think that if we are not hard on ourselves or punishing ourselves over our failures and flaws, we risk a runaway ego and fall into the traps of false pride.

Take for example, Norman. A young bank executive who is also a new father. Between juggling work and a new baby, he also spends time volunteering as a football coach at a local shelter. He is a committed father and husband, a hard worker and a community role-model. But Norman has gone through several episodes of anxiety attacks simply because he feels overwhelmed, he feels he isn't contributing enough in his team at work and isn't good enough as a husband or father.

People have misgivings about self-compassion and it is only because nobody really knows what it looks like, or even how to practice it so it doesn't become excessive and borderline narcissistic. Self compassion has the element of mindfulness, of wisdom and the recognition to common humanity. Research by Kristin Neff points the myths that people have on self-compassion is the main reason why most of us are in the cycle of criticizing yourself over and over again. Here are the common myths:

#1 Self-Compassion is just a person crying out for self-pity
Let's get this straight- self compassion does not mean you are feeling sorry for

yourself. It is fact an antidote to self-pity. It isn't about whining about our bad luck but instead, self-compassion makes us more open to acknowledging. accepting and experiencing difficult feelings with the help of kindness. Self-compassionate people have a lower tendency of wallowing in self-pity about how bad the circumstances may be and this leads to better mental clarity and mental health.

Filip Raes of the University of Leuven conducted a study on the connection between self-compassion, mental health and ruminative thinking. This study was conducted among the students in his university. Students were first assessed using the Self-Compassion Scale developed by Dr. Kristin Neff. Participants were asked how often they responded to behaviors that corresponded with the main components of self-compassion. These behaviors included "I try to be patient and understanding towards the elements of my personality that I am not fond of"; "When things are going badly for me, I see them as part of life that happens to everyone".

The result of the study showed that students who had better self-compassion parameters were less whiny and broody when things did not go their way. They were also less anxious and less depressed and showed better signs of attentiveness.

#2 Self-compassion is a sign of weakness

Melissa, as a first born child was always seen as the responsible one, a label she has taken on with pride. She sees herself as a pillar of strength to her family. However, since Melissa got married, she has decided to take a step back and pay more attention to her new marriage. While her own family has never imposed on her, Melissa secretly feels as if she is not being a good daughter, and racked with guilt. When her friends suggested that she try not being too hard on herself, her reaction was to immediately tell them off, saying that self-compassion does not make her a good daughter. What Melissa does not know is that this is not a sign of her abandoning her family or a sign of weakness but discovering self-compassion is part of the process of resilience to us. When going through changes in life, self-compassion enables us to survive and thrive.

#3 Self-Compassion can make you a complacent person

Thinking that self-compassion makes you complacent is one of the biggest blocks you can place on yourself. It's so easy for us to criticize ourselves just because we fail to live up to certain standards and we immediately label ourselves as sloths. Do we do this to our kids too?

Amanda's daughter just failed her Biology test and upon finding out, Amanda starts berating her, saying that she is stupid and that she is ashamed of her. This is the exact same thing that Amanda tells herself when she fails to live up to a certain expectation. Rather than motivating her daughter, these comments on her daughter lose faith in herself and prevents her from trying to do better.

What Amanda can do however is practice a more compassionate approach to the situation by giving a hug, telling her daughter that it happens to anyone and what support can she give her daughter. Telling her daughter that she believes in her will help motivate her.

Amanda needs to give honest recognition to the failure as well as empathize with her daughter's unhappiness. This caring response helps us boost out self-confidence and spread emotional support.

While Amanda may not have said those words to her daughter, she still believes deep down that this type of negative feedback may spur her daughter to achieve the necessary goals. But thanks research on human emotions and its responses, showing self-compassion is more effective to boost a better rate of success than self-punishment.

Juliana Breines and Serena Chen of University of California conducted a research to examine the effects of self-compassion and to see how or if it was one of the factors that motivated participants to get involved in positive behaviors and make positive changes. Participants were ask to think back at a time when they felt guilty about such as lying to a partner, cheating in an exam which made them feel bad even till now. They were then randomly assigned to write to themselves from three different perspectives:

1. that of a compassionate and understanding friend
2. write about their own positive qualities
3. write about a hobby they enjoyed doing

Researchers found that participants involved in the self-compassionate perspective were more remorseful for their wrong doing and were more motivated to not repeat the offence.

The research concluded that self-compassion was not about evading personal accountability, rather strengthening it. Acknowledging our failures with kindness rather than judgements enables us to see ourselves clearly beyond the spectacles of self-judgement. Tell ourselves 'I can't believe I messed up. I got so stressed and I overreacted' rather than 'I cannot believe i said that. Why am I so mean?'

#4 Self-Compassions makes us more narcissistic

To many Americans, having high self-esteem means that you are special and beyond average. For some people with high self-esteem, the minute that we receive a less than average score, our self-esteem crashes and plummets. There is no way that everyone to be above average all the time. There are some areas that we can excel because we are naturally good at it but then there are aspects that we either under perform or we are just average. That is why diversity is good. At times when we do perform below average, we see ourselves like failures. The desire to be above average is always going to be there, as we like that feeling of high self-esteem. However this can make us be develop nasty behaviors.

Jean Twenge, a researcher from the San Diego University and Keith Campbell from the University of Georgia have been studying narcissism scores since 1987 among college students. It may not come as a surprise to you to know that among modern-day social media savvy students, narcissism ran high.

It is extremely important to note the difference between self-compassion and self-esteem. While they are both connected to our psychological well-being, the difference is very vivid:

- Self-esteem is evaluating your self-worth positively
- Self-compassion is relating to the changes that happen to us with kindness and acceptance

With self-esteem, we want to feel better than the people around us but with self-compassion, we acknowledge the fact that we have and share certain imperfections. Self-esteem is buoyancy, depending on our latest success or failure. Those with higher levels of self-esteem tend to get upset when they receive neutral feedback. They often start thinking 'Am I just average? I thought i was exceptional'. They are also likelier to listen to any feedback that is related to their personality and blame it on external factors. Self-esteem thrives only when the reviews are good which leads to evasiveness.

Self-compassionate people on the other hand are more emotionally stable despite the degree of praise they receive.

#5 Self-compassion makes us selfish
It is easy to conflate self-compassion with selfishness. Joshua for example spends a large portion of his day caring for his family and at weekends, he supports activities at the local college. He was raised in a family placed importance on service to others. This eventually led him to think that spending time for self-care

and being kind and caring to his needs meant he must be neglecting the people around him just for his own needs.

There are plenty of people like Joshua- selfless, good, altruistic and generous to others but horrible to their own selves. When we become too absorbed in self-judgement, we end up giving less because we are preoccupied by thinking about our inadequacies and worthless selves.

Plenty of our emotional needs are met when we are kind and nurturing to ourselves which leaves us in a better position to focus on the people around us. However, caring for the welfare of others often becomes a bigger priority and the idea of treating ourselves badly starts rearing its ugly head.Think about the safety message on an airplane. It is advised to place the oxygen mask over your ownself before assisting others right? This is the same for self compassion.

Kristin Neff conducted a research with Tasha Beretvas of the University of Texas just to prove that being good to ourselves is more helpful when we want to be good to others. The research look at whether people who were self-compassionate were more giving in their relationships.It explored 100 couple who are in romantic relationships for a year or longer. Participants were asked to rate themselves based on the Self-Compassion Scale.

Neff & Beretvas found that partners who were self-compassionate individuals were described as more accepting, caring and supportive compared to self-critical partners who were seen as detached, controlling and aggressive. Self-compassionate partners brought to the table a more secure and satisfied relationship.

A growing research also focuses on therapists and caregivers who were more self-compassionate. Those who were were less likely to feel caregiver burnout and they were more satisfied with their careers, they were more happy, they felt more energized and were more grateful to be able to make a difference.

Conclusion

Self-compassion enables us to feel love, courage, wisdom and generosity in a more sustainable way. It gives us a boundless and directionless mental and emotional state. The power of self-compassion can be enriched through practice and of course through learning, just like so many other good habits.

Being kind to ourselves is not a selfish luxury or a sign of weakness or self-pity. It is a gift to our persons to make us happier and more fulfilled. Thanks to the many research conducted, we now know the myths of self-compassion.

Chapter 4- Dealing with Negativity

Did you ever realize that it is much easier to be happy than it is to be unhappy? Go ahead. Think about it. While you are reading this, just think about the many things that happened before you opening this book and reading. What happened when you woke up? Did you get a kiss from your partner? How did your coffee taste this morning? How is the weather outside like now? All these things that happened to you today, what made you happy and what made you sad?

If you listed ten things today and 7 of them were things that made your happy and three made you unhappy, sad, frustrated or moody, then most likely you were grateful, and you were positive. The thing is, many of us would prefer to be happy and positive rather than be unhappy and negative. And it is that simple to be positive and happy. Also, positive thinking is above and beyond just being happy or displaying a cheerful and upbeat attitude. It also creates and establishes value in your life and relationships, and it also helps you build skills that benefit you longer than your smile can take you. Barbara Fredrickson, a positive psychology researcher from the University of North Carolina, published a landmark paper on the impact of positive thinking on work, health and general wellbeing. Here's a little brief of Barbara's research:

What Can Negative Thinking do to your Brain?

Our brain is programmed to respond to negative emotions by shutting off the world around us and limiting the options we see around us. For example, if you get into a fight with your sister, your emotions and anger might consume to the point where you react adversely- you can't think about anything else. Or for instance your coffee this morning spilled on your shirt, and this creates a domino effect of everything going wrong in your day, and you get so stressed out that you find it hard to start or do anything because you've lost your focus. Or if you are supposed to complete a project but you didn't, you start to feel bad about it and all you think is how irresponsible you are and that you are lazy, and you lack motivation. The point is, our brain shuts off from the outside world and relies on the negative emotions of fear, stress, and anger. Negative thoughts and emotions prevent us from seeing other options, solutions or choices that are around us.

What Can Positive Thinking do to your Brain?

Barbara Fredrickson also explains how positive thinking manifests in our brain. She explains with an experiment where research subjects are divided into five groups, and each group is shown a different video clip. The first group was shown clips that created feelings of joy whereas the second group was shown clips that created contentment, the third was the control group that had images of no significant emotions and were neutral whereas group four had clips that created fear and group five had clips that created the feelings of anger.

Participants were then asked to imagine themselves in situations that these same emotions would come about and write down their reactions to it. Participants that viewed images of fear and anger had the least responses or reactions whereas participants who saw joy and contentment had more reactions. The bottom line is, if you experience positive emotions you will see more possibilities in life. Positive emotions broaden our possibilities and thinking, thus opening up more options for us in facing issues, crisis, problems, and solutions and so on. In the next few chapters, we will discuss how we can work our mind to be more positive and look at things in a more positive perspective to enhance and give more value to our life, relationships, and goals. It is not as hard as it seems because all it takes is a little practice.

Have you seen the movie Inside Out?

If you did, then you will probably realize that being sad is a good thing- not always, but this emotion is there for a reason. When we talk about dealing with negativity, it doesn't necessarily mean being optimistic all the time, especially in the face of suffering.

Pain and sadness are just part of the complex human emotions all of us have, and it is just as important to feel pain and sadness, guilt and fear as this are all part and parcel of coping. Experiencing and processing negative emotions in a healthy way is a crucial part of personal growth.

There are two scenarios when people are confronted with negative situations. One, they either obsess over the problem or two, they numb their emotions. Either of these coping methods is not healthy, and it can create harmful patterns in our mind, over a period of time. Obsessing is deceptive because it feels as if you are thinking things through but to continuously obsess over a situation only reinforces the impact of the negative thoughts and emotions.

That said, numbing your emotions towards a pained situation isn't good either because it really is not possible to selectively numb out an emotion. Humans are so complex that our range of emotions does not enable us to directly shut down an emotion. If you somehow blot out anger, you'll blur out happiness and serenity too. Why? Because while you like being active and optimistic all the time, not showing anger to something that has hurt you or pained you or frustrated you, will make you feel more bitter eventually. Only because you weren't able to express your anger, the situation or the person related to this will not know how you feel. For example, if we use alcohol to numb our pain, we do not learn how to cope with sadness. We just develop another problem which is alcohol abuse.

If you are going through a pained time, then you need to develop healthy coping skills, and this involves recognizing the inevitability and necessity of some suffering and moving on from it. The process usually includes:

- Acknowledging your negative feelings and watch them with a non-judgmental attitude

- Recognize when they are triggered and assess your reactions when responding to this
- Understand that pain is just a catalyst for growth and resilience
- Practice forgiveness towards those who have pained you
- Express yourself in creative and healthy ways like painting or exercising
- Seek the support of others

Steps to deal with Negative thoughts and Events

Here are some tried and tested ways to overcome negative thoughts and events which you can try:

1. Meditate or do yoga.

Yoga helps take your focus away from your thoughts and bring attention to your breath. Yoga or meditation is very relaxing, and it helps ease one's mind. It also helps you stay present and focused on the moment that is happening.

2. Smile.

Pain and sadness can make it very hard to smile. While it does seem hard to smile when you aren't feeling so happy inside, you need to sometimes force this out of you. So try doing this in front of a mirror everyday or make a mental note to smile to the people you correspond with daily.

3. Surround yourself with positive people.

Surround yourself with friends and family that can give you constructive and loving feedback. Each time you feel you are going down into your negative spiral, call these people up and speak to them so they can put your focus back again to where it's needed to be at the time.

4. Change your thoughts from negative to positive.

Easier said than done, no doubt but you can turn any situation into a positive one. For example, if you have just started a new job you barely have enough experience of, instead of saying 'I'll take a long time to adjust or learn' just say 'I will take on any challenges because challenges excite me!'

5. *Don't wallow in self-pity. Take charge of your life*

You are the captain of your shop so do not make yourself a victim. There is always a way out of any situation so if it becomes to unbearable, then leave. Otherwise, you stay put and make the best of it and don't point fingers, blame, complain or whine.

6. *Volunteer*

Volunteering also takes the focus away. If you think you are in a bad situation, imagine the people who need food aid or money. Do something nice for someone else so volunteer at an organization or donate.

7. *Remember to keep moving forward*

We easily dwell on our mistakes and feel terrible for the way we acted. But you can't reverse the situation so instead of feeling sorry for yourself or beating yourself up over what you'd done, tell yourself that you'd made a mistake, you learned from it, and you want to move on.

8. *Listen to music*

One of the best ways to alleviate your mood especially in the morning is by listening to songs and singing in the shower! It doesn't matter if you remember the lyrics – a good happy song will put you in a good and happy mood.

9. *Be grateful*

Being grateful enables you to appreciate all the things you have. So be grateful every day.

10. Read positive quotes.

Just log into Pinterest, read positive quotes every day. Better yet, print out the ones that you like and stick in on your wall, your fridge or your computer.

Learn to Forgive Yourself

Just like negative emotions, failure is also good to experience because it only makes us stronger.

Yes! Failure is something that didn't kill you. You're still alive! So what doesn't kill you only makes you stronger. Why do you need experience failure? Nobody wants to experience failure but if you looked at the successful people in our generation today, or even the past- they all failed. They all made mistakes. They all went through trial and error. What sets them apart from the perennial failures? They didn't give up. They learnt from their mistakes. They had extreme passion, making them eager to keep on trying till they succeeded. Here's why you need to experience failure:

Without failure, you'd be sucked into a blissful feeling that nothing can go wrong and that everything you'd put into place will work exactly as how it should be

When something does go wrong, you are unable to cope with the change or adapt to create solutions.

Failure enables us to work on our flaws and it also allows us to right our wrongs. Failure also enables us upgrade or enhance or refine our work, technique and solutions

Failure also teaches us a lesson. It is our choice to learn from it or run from it

When we fail, it's easy to get discouraged and upset and we develop a sense of being afraid to fail again. In order to be successful in anything that we do, we just need to remind ourselves to let go of our pride and ego. Failure only makes us grow wiser, make us more adaptable and vivid to any possible scenarios that could happen. We are more prepared to face the same problem but at a different angle.

So how do you look at failure at a positive way? We need to redefine the way we view failure. The fear of failure is what stops many great individuals from creating something beneficial and meaningful in our world. The fear of failure is why we stop ourselves from living extraordinary lives.

The fear of failure is why we never submitted the novel we wrote, we never expressed our feelings to the people we love, never bungee jumped or telling someone how you really feel.

Daniel Epstein, founder of Unreasonable group stresses the point of re-branding the way we see failure. He suggests defining it as such:

"To Fail means "to not start doing something you believe in. To stop doing something you believe in just because it is hard. To ignore your gut instinct around what you believe is right and wrong."

In actual fact, many of the world's greatest philosophers, entrepreneurs, scientists and artisans have all expressed their thoughts on failure and how it has helped them overcome adversity and obstacles. All these perceptions tell us that fear of failure is evident in every human being but with passion and perseverance to achieve what you want will be the driving force in the determination between constant failure and success.

Hopefully, these quotes will give you a good perspective. After all, what better way to learn than to be inspired by some of the most successful people on earth?

Remembering that I'll be dead soon is the most important tool I've ever encountered to help me make the big choices in life. Because almost everything – all external expectations, all pride, all fear of embarrassment or failure – these things just fall away in the face of death, leaving only what is truly important. ~Steve Jobs

I've missed more than 9000 shots in my career. I've lost almost 300 games. 26 times, I've been trusted to take the game winning shot and missed. I've failed over and over and over again in my life. And that is why I succeed. ~Michael Jordan

Our doubts are traitors, and make us lose the good we oft might win, by fearing to attempt. ~William Shakespeare

For every failure, there's an alternative course of action. You just have to find it. When you come to a roadblock, take a detour. ~Mary Kay Ash

Failure is blindness to the strategic element in events; success is readiness for instant action when the opportune moment arrives. ~Newell D. Hillis

The only real failure in life is not to be true to the best one knows. ~Buddha

Success is often achieved by those who don't know that failure is inevitable. ~Coco Chanel

Steps to Overcome Failure

Highly successful people are the ones who have failed the most. We only hear about their successes but never the trials and tribulations and obstacles that they had to go through. Setbacks and failures are part of life and nobody is perfect. Yes we fall into hard times at some point in our lives but what this is all a lesson to us. If we can manage it effectively, then no matter what comes our way in the future, we can overcome it. Here are four steps that can help you turn any negative experience into a positive one:

- **Failure is part of the road to success**

When times get tough, the tough get going. It is frustrating to hear people tell us to be positive when we are faced with adversity but this doesn't mean we have to be smiling all the time or be happy all the time. Staying positive is knowing that despite your setback, you can bounce back again. Staying positive is learning and growing and evolving. Understand that setbacks aren't the end of the road; rather it is carving a step in our journey to succeed. When life hits you with a setback, its okay to be sad and frustrated and upset- but we should never stay down.

- **Blow your Steam off**

When you hit a setback or a failure, your mind gets clouded. You worked so hard to get to this point, only to fail. If you have come to this point, take a step back and evaluate your work. Take some time off to clear your head and accept your mistakes. Once you have done this, you will begin to accept what has happened and how it happened or why it happened. This emotional state will eventually evaporate and then you can go back to focus on the work at hand.

- **Be Honest**

Being brutally honest to ourselves in the midst of a failure is a trait of success. Most people do not want to admit their mistake or admit that it is their own fault that all these negative scenarios have happened. The thing is, part of being positive is also about being responsible and being accountable to ourselves and the mistakes we have made. We need to do this because this is how we learn. Albert Einstein once said that it is crazy to keep doing the same thing over and over again and expecting different results. That is why learning from our mistakes is a crucial part of moving on and part of learning. If we do not learn from our mistakes, we are doomed to be repeating them again and again and again.

- **Move Forward**

We need to move forward each time we fail. When we fail, we fail forward which means learning from our setbacks and then, making the necessary adjustments until we reach success. You have come so far, do not give up. So each change we make, each person we meet and every tiny bit of information we learn all combines to create a different outcome for us to learn from.

Obstacles are inevitable in life but there are always two ways of handling them. While they may block your focus out temporarily, our perseverance is the element that determines whether we fall back or move forward. As we get more and more efficient in the journey of positive thinking, we will enable ourselves to always see the positive side of things even in the most darkest of situations or the hardest of times.

Surrounding yourself with Positive People

No doubt that people have a huge impact on your life. According to Jim Rohn, American entrepreneur and motivation speaker, we all spend our time with an average of five people. With this in mind, think about who these 5 people are and how they impact your life.

Some people, including your friends whom you've known for a long time, can be parasites. These parasites suck out your energy and happiness and even your resources.

So what makes someone a 'good' person you can spend your time with? What are the benefits of surrounding yourself with self-disciplined people?

Your GOOD Category

The people around you can be good in so many ways. This doesn't mean that they go to church every Sunday. It's more like feeding the poor, looking after abandon dogs or something simple like encouraging you to hit the gym more often. These people can be your friends, your family, your co-workers and even some acquaintances.

In essence, good people are productive people. They have a lot of good traits in them that inspire and motivate you too.

It is also important to note too much of something good can also inhibit your growth. You need diversity and healthy arguments and discussions along the way. Always be eager to learn new knowledge and look at different perspectives from your peers.

Think About How You Interact with People

Time for a little exercise. Write down the names of the five people you usually spend time with. Then, write down the qualities you see in them. Think about how they positively or negatively affect you. Are you happy around them? Do they make you feel like you got what it takes to reach your goals? Do they support you? If your list has more positives than negatives, then you probably have the good people around you.

You want to surround yourself with people who make you happy, with those that make you feel alive, the people who help you when you are in need and those that make you feel safe- they are the ones who genuinely care and are worth keeping in your life.

The key here is to finding what is good for you because what is good for you may be different for someone else.

So how do you do that?

Your vibe is what will attract the people around you. When you give off good vibes, good vibes will follow you. You will also feel less stressed and find joy even in the most simplest things like the blue sky or a scoop of vanilla ice cream.

So train your mind to not think negatively and try to see the positive side of things. It is ok to feel sadness and grief and bitterness when things don't go the way you want or something bad happens but if you start building a home in the negativity scene, it'll be harder for you to leave it.

Today, make a commitment to start spending more time with the good people in your life.

Benefits of surrounding yourself with Positive People
1.   You Do not get into needless battles

Thoughts become things- you've heard it before. But some of these things are also feelings and feelings are energy. The feelings of happiness, sadness, gratitude, confidence are all energy- negative and positive. When you surround yourself with positive people, you eliminate negative energy, thus eliminate unnecessary conflicts.

You get to live in the feeling of gratitude more frequently

People who are happy will genuinely be happy for you when you make it big or achieve your goal. Surrounding yourself with unsuccessful people and then talking about your successes will only remind these people of what they don't have. By contrast, surrounding yourself with people that have more than what you have you will make you feel more gratitude frequently. Gratitude is the attitude that brings success.

For example, if you achieved your goal in achieving a healthy, physically toned body, you're not going to be telling this to someone who is overweight (by choice) right? Because that person will only think you are bragging and wont share in your good fortune.

2. You get to be someone you've never been

In order to do something you have never done before, you need to stop caring about what people think of you. You need to realize that you cannot be doing the same things you have done if you want to become someone better. Surrounding yourself with people who want to achieve the same goal as you can make you do things you otherwise will not do. Successful people recognize that change is inevitable and that it must take place. Unsuccessful people will begrudge the changes in you whereas successful people will be glad that it happened and welcome it.

Chapter 5: Building and Mastering Emotions

Being aware of our emotions also means knowing that our emotions can drive our behavior and impact those around us, either positively or negatively. It also means we have the ability to manage these emotions, that of our own and that of others, especially at pressuring and stressful times.

The Five Categories of Emotional Intelligence (EQ)

When it comes to Emotional Intelligence, there are five categories that becomes a focus.

1. **Self-awareness.**

Having self-awareness means having the ability to recognize an emotion as and when it occurs and it is the key to your EQ. In order to develop self-awareness, a person needs to tune into their own true feelings, evaluating them and subsequently managing them.

In self-awareness, the important elements are:

- Recognizing our own own emotions and its effects
- Having a level of confidence and sureness of your capabilities and your self-worth

2. **Self-regulation.**

When we experience emotions, we often have little control over our actions when we first feel these emotions. One thing we can control however is how long these emotions last. To control how long certain emotions last, especially negative ones, certain methods are used to lessen the effects of these emotions such as anxiety, anger and even depression. These methods include reinventing a scenario in a much positive manner such as through taking a long walk, saying a prayer and even meditating.

Self-regulation includes:

- Innovation which means open to new ideas
- Adaptability to handle change and be flexible
- Trustworthiness referring to the ability to keep to standards of integrity and honesty
- Taking responsibility, conscientiousness of our own actions
- Self-control to prevent disruptive impulses

3. Motivation

Having motivation is what keeps us going to accomplish our tasks and goals and to maintain an air of positivity. With practice and with effort, we can all program our minds to be more positive although as human beings, it is also good to be negative at times. This does not mean having negative thoughts are bad, but these thoughts need to be kept in check as they cause more harm than good. Whenever you feel like you have negative feelings, you can also reprogram them to be more positive or at least to pick out the positive aspects of the situation, the silver lining which will help you be more focused in solving the problem.

Motivation is made up of:

- Having the sense of achievement drive, to constantly strive to improve and meet a level of excellence.
- Having the commitment to align your individual, group or organizational goals
- Having the initiative to act on available opportunities
- Having the optimism to pursue your goals persistently and objectively, despite the setbacks and obstacles.

4. Empathy

Empathy is the ability to recognize how people would feel towards a certain scenario, thing or person. Having this ability is crucial to success both in career as with life. The more you can decipher the feelings of people, the better you can manage the thoughts and approaches you send them. Empathetic people are excellent at:

- Recognizing, anticipating and meeting a person's needs
- Developing the needs of other people and bolstering their individual abilities
- Taking advantage of diversity by cultivating opportunities among different people
- Developing political awareness by understanding the current emotional state of people and fostering powerful relationships
- Focusing on identifying feelings and wants of other people

5. Social skills.

Developing good interpersonal skills is imperative as well if you want a successful life and a successful career. In our world today when plenty of thing are digitized, social skills seem to be an afterthought. People skills are more relevant and sought-after then before especially since now you also need a high EQ understand, negotiate and empathize with others especially if you deal and interact with different people on a daily basis. Among the most useful skills are:

- Influence to effectively wield persuasive tactics
- Communication to send our clear and concise messages
- Leadership to inspire and guide people and groups.
- Change catalyst in kick-starting and managing change
- Managing conflicting situations which includes the ability to negotiate, understand and resolve disagreements

74

- To bond and nurture meaningful and instrumental relationships
- Teamwork, cooperation and collaboration in meeting shared goals
- Creating a synergetic group to work towards collective goals.

Creating a Balance with Emotional Awareness

As a human being, emotions and feelings make up every aspect of our existence. Managing them and keeping them balanced will help us reach our maximum potential in life, at work and especially in our relationships. As we know by now, having good emotional balance leads us towards better physical and mental health, making life happier.

When our emotional well-being is disrupted, this will result in the opposite. Our physical health will decline, we will start having digestive problems, lack of energy and sleep issues. People with emotional distress often exhibit low self-esteem, they are self-critical and pessimistic. They always need to assert themselves through their behavior. They are overly worried, get afraid very fast and they are focused on the past.

- Connection between our Thoughts and Feelings

Thoughts determine our feelings and they are nothing more than firing the neurons in our body. Our thoughts also generate feelings, making our body release additive natural substances such as cortisol and adrenaline.

The connection between the body and the mind is extremely vivid and strong, strong enough that the mental and physical state sends positive and negative vibes both ways. The feelings we experience depends on our thought, combined with our attitudes and actions.

Emotions are part of our daily life and we experience this everyday. What we want is to strike a balance in our emotions, thoughts and feelings to ensure that they do not adversely affect our daily tasks and cause us stress.

- **Creating Emotional Balance**

So how we do create emotional balance? Emotional balance is the ability to maintain equilibrium and flexibility between the mind and body when we are faced with changes or challenges. Here are some ways that you can create emotional balance:

1. Accept your emotions

Many of our mental, emotional and physical problems stem from our inability to express ourselves emotionally. When we experience an emotional distraught, we smother it in the comforts of eating, sleeping, sweating it out, sucking it up, it is swept under a rug, we bury it, project it elsewhere, meditate even all in the hopes of suppressing our emotions instead of actually dealing with it by accepting that this is what we are going through right not. The key here is to allow ourselves unconditional permission to feel- to cry when we want to, to feel anger when we are angry, sadness when we grief and so on. Let your guard down either when you are alone or with someone you trust and just focus on the feeling and situation. Experience and immerse yourself in this feeling so you can comprehend better why it hurts and what you will be doing to remedy the situation once you've accepted and acknowledge these feelings.

2. Express yourself

Expressing yourself is important. There are many ways to express oneself and usually when we experience a feeling, we react by crying, shouting, throwing things. But to identify with ourselves and be able to manage our emotions properly, we can also express ourselves through more positive ways. Some people like reading as it provides an escape into a different world. Some people express themselves through art or music. Whatever it is that you do, make sure you stay connected to discover more about yourself, your identity and also the person you want to become.

3. Don't shove your feelings

Sometimes, it is easy to shove our feelings and not think about it, especially painful and scary memories. But as we all know, stuffing your memories and feelings will only make things worse for you. While it is hard to address your fears and sadness, rage and anger, once you actually dive into it, you will find that it will become easier to face your fears and eventually, the choppy waters will become calmer.

Be accepting your past and dealing with it in a more emotional state, you ultimately will lead a harmonious life. Always allow yourself to feel because your reactions to these different feelings would be in a more stable way rather than an overreaction.

4. See the world in a positive light

It is easier said than done, we know. In a world full of hatred, sadness, grief, war, crime, unfairness- it is a threat to our emotional health. You tend to develop low self-esteem and start asking yourself if you are worth it, if you can get through it, if you are doing things right and all these thinking steers you towards making more mistakes and missteps. Rather than having emotional self-doubt, take action to develop a prerogative of seeing the world in a more positive light.

Do not feel responsible for the bad things that happen which is not caused by you is a good start. Have compassion in yourself and practice mindfulness and accept that occasional lapses and failures are just part of being human.

5. Get a grip on your mind

The way we think causes us emotional distress- this probably is not news to you.

We all have this tendency into overthinking and these thoughts that do not serve you or give you any positivity is just setting you up for emotional distress. So get a grip on your mind- do not let it wander to much especially when you start overthinking.

6. Practice Yoga and Mindfulness

Doing yoga on a daily basis does help in your mental health- it helps by increasing your confidence in your abilities and it also helps you make better, definitive decisions.

You also learn to not be so self-criticizing. Yoga, practiced on a daily basis can help get rid of negative energy within you and help you work your way towards mental clarity and vital energy.

Not only that, the breathing that is practiced in yoga helps you relax better, make you calmer especially if your mind is racing and it also helps you to refine your feelings.

Breathing correctly helps you get rid of stress and anxiety as well.

Conclusion

While emotional balance is vital, just remember that it is alright to have emotional imbalance so do not beat yourself up over it and overthink things. However, do not neglect this imbalance. If you feel you are emotionally imbalanced, do something about it either talk to someone you trust, meet a therapist or just find a positive way to express your emotions and feelings. Live a life without or little regrets.

Chapter 6: Practical steps for Becoming self compassionate

Self-compassion is necessary for a healthy relationship, healthy mind and healthy body. How we interact with people and how we think affects how our body responds too. Self-compassion is the practice of goodwill and not good feelings. To practice self-compassion, we have first and foremost, change the way we think and perceive things. We also need a little bit of faith and believe in ourselves, in our strengths, in the way our life is heading, our goals and our priorities.

In this chapter, we will look at:

- the power of faith and believe in changing our perceptions
- practising creative visualization
- Practising affirmations

- **Faith & Believe**

When someone says 'Have faith' this depends on what you view or think what faith is. For many people, faith can be many different things and in all honesty, there's no right or wrong.

Conventionally, a lot of people associate faith with spirituality or the faith in God and that's not wrong either but like mentioned above, the very fact that people have different perspectives of what faith is is a good thing! It is quite enlightening and helpful to plenty of individuals that faith has different meanings as it can help different people make clearer sense of the various spectrums of life.

Here's a quick guideline to what faith means:

- **Faith**

Faith can mean faith in a supreme being, in God. But psychologists of religion would say that this is more of belief. Faith, in a more naturalistic and psychological sense, is really about the innate sense to search for meaning, purpose, and significance. Every human person has a strong sense that there is more than what meets the eye. In other words, there is something more than just 'me' and as human beings, we all discover what this might be- some of us go all out while some of us are content with the information we have at the moment.

All of us human beings seek out to find the deeper meaning, purpose and significance that exist in our lives, in our relationships and all the things that occur around us. This is the very basic striving of faith and the universal role it plays in our lives.

Wikipedia describes faith as a trust or confidence on a person, element or thing. Faith also is connected to the observation of an obligatory process that creates loyalty or even fidelity to a person, a promise or engagement. Faith is also a belief that is not based on facts and proof and faith can also mean loyalty to a system of religious belief.

While we think that only people that belief in divine intervention or God seem to have faith, the thing is even atheists have this kind of faith- a belief or trust or confidence. Everyone has the gift of faith- some of us have strong faith while some of us have weaker faith, but it really depends on the context we talk about.

- Belief

This brings us to the next element- belief. Belief is a representation of truth claims that you make on your spiritual journey. Beliefs are what tell you what is true and what is not true, and this is based on your experiences to satisfy your sense of faith. Your beliefs are what your hold to be true in your journey to satisfy your faith by engaging in various spiritual pursuits such as pilgrimage.

- **The Value of Faith**

While we all like to think we have faith (and high levels of it) the truth is, the value of our faith only grows when we are faced with troubling times. Many people believe that their faith value is determined by the evidence of things or successful moments or achievements in life. But the value of faith only increases as we grow older, as we experience more and more things in life, some good and some bad. Our faith becomes more valuable as we go through the trials and testaments of life and its heartaches. It is only during these times that you truly understand the depth and strength of a person's faith.

- **The Difference between Faith & Belief**

Probably by reading this now, you'd come to deduce that faith and belief are not the same things. In fact, in most cases, faith and belief are entirely the opposite of each other. Confusion between these two elements is tested when you face a crisis. While you may be searching for faith in something at a moment of crisis, you may be only pulling out the various beliefs that you have.

So the question is, who are you if not for your convictions?

If you have gone through a terrible crisis in life, you are probably still trying to figure it all out. Some people take years to understand why what happened to them, happened. Many people, especially those who are religious, feel the need to leave their faith in God because they believe that God has abandoned them.

But the questions are, were you abandoned by God or were you abandoned by your beliefs?

- **Belief as a product of the Mind**

A negative mind is already at a disadvantage but even a healthy mind can run into its own set of problems. For the enabled mind, a person may think that because they pray to God, all their prayers will be answered and that God is just and he will set things right. The positive mind will say that if we hold on to our beliefs strongly, God listens and will favor us.

But what is it that we believe in? Our beliefs are rooted in our culture and our upbringing. This is the first thing that separates our faith from our belief. Oftentimes, what we belief in may directly contradict everything else we know to be true and right. It can be universally acknowledged that we arrive at the crossroads of faith and belief when we go through a life-threatening crisis ourselves and when this happens, we end up changing our stronghold beliefs.

Changing our minds to adapt to crises is to change some part or elements of our beliefs. It is perfectly normal to shift our beliefs because our beliefs are modeled on personal and communal experience. A belief can necessarily be not true even when it has been handed down to us. In other words, a belief is not necessarily the only truth.

- **Belief is a product of the mind, faith is not**

Faith is the product of the spirit. Our mind also has a tendency to interfere with the process of faith rather than contributing it. To have confidence in the most depressing of times will require us to quiet the mind because the mind can run amok when we let it, especially when we have every negative thought clouding our mind.

Faith comes in when our beliefs run aground. Be wary that our beliefs can sway our spirit. Think of Galileo and how everyone thought the world was flat until he came around to prove that the world was indeed round. The belief that we humans have held for centuries can come and go over the course of a millennium.

- **Beliefs come and go**

But our faith is not as fickle as our belief. True faith is not a statement of our beliefs, but it is a state of being. Faith is trusting beyond all reasonable doubt and beyond all evidence that you have not been abandoned. Faith is achieved through commitment and to commit to faith is not the same thing as committing to a series of beliefs. When we are in the moment of crisis, faith tells us it doesn't matter whether its God or circumstances. To not know in the perspective of faith is to remain humble and open to learning. When faith does not fill in the cracks in a crisis, then fear will. Therefore, faith is an attitude that we create where it is the acceptance of not knowing. Unknowing is what creates faith.

Practicing Creative Visualization to Encourage Self-Compassion

Creative visualization is a mental technique that harnesses our imagination to make our goals and dreams a reality. When used the right way, creative visualization has been proven to improve the lives of the people who have used it, and it also increases the success and prosperity rate of the individual. Creative visualization unleashes a power that can alter your social and living environment and circumstances, it causes beneficial events to happen, attracts positivity in work, life, relationships, and goals.

Creative visualization is not a magic potion. It uses the cognitive processes of our mind to purposely generate an array of visual mental imagery to create beneficial physiological, psychological or social effects such as increasing wealth, healing wounds to the body or alleviating psychological issues such as anxiety and sadness. This method uses the power of the mind to attract good energy and really, it is the magic potion behind every success.

Mostly, a person needs to visualize an individual event or situation or object or desire to attract it into their lives. This is a process that is similar to daydreaming. It only uses the natural process of the power of our mind to initiate positive thoughts and natural mental laws. Successful people like Oprah and Tiger Woods and Bill Gates use this technique, either consciously or unconsciously, attracting success and positive outcomes into their lives by visualizing their goals as already attained or accomplished.

- **The Power of Thoughts and Creative Visualization**

So how does this work and why is it so important to us?

Well, our mind is a powerful thing. With only the power of our mind, we can reach amazing success, or we can also spiral out of control. It swings both ways. Our subconscious mind accepts the ideals and thoughts that we often repeat, and when our mind accepts it, then your mindset also changes accordingly, and this influences your habits and actions. Again, a domino effect happens where you end up meeting new people or getting into situations or circumstances that lead you to your goal. Our thoughts come with a creative power that can mold our life and attract whatever we think about.

Remember the saying that goes 'mind over matter?' When we set our mind to do it, our body does what our mind tells us. Our thoughts travel from mind, body, and soul but believe it or not; it can travel from one mind to another because it is unconsciously picked up by the people you meet with every day and usually, most of the people you end up meeting are the ones who can help you achieve your goals.

You probably think and repeat certain thoughts everyday pretty often, and you probably do this consciously or unconsciously. You probably have focused your thoughts on your current situation or environment and subsequently, create and recreate the same events and circumstances regularly. While most of our lives are somewhat routine, we can always change these thoughts by visualizing different circumstances and situations, and in a way, create a different reality for you to focus on new goals and desires.

- **Changing Your Reality**

Honestly, though, you can change your 'reality by changing your thoughts and mental images. You aren't creating magic here; all you are doing is harnessing the natural powers and laws that inhibit each and every one of us. The thing that separates normal, average folk with wildly successful people is that the successful ones have mastered their thoughts and mental images while the rest of us are still learning or trying to cope. Changing your thoughts and attitude changes and reshapes your world.

Take for example you plan on moving into a larger apartment and instead of wallowing in self-pity such as the lack of money, do this instead- alter your thoughts and attitude and visualize yourself living in a larger apartment. It isn't difficult to do because it's exactly like daydreaming.

- **Overcoming Limited Thinking**

You may think daydreaming about positive things and money and success and great relationships are nothing but child's play but in fact, creative visualization can do wonders. Though that, it may be hard for different individuals to immediate alter their thoughts. Limits to this positive thinking are within us and not the power of our mind- we control it.

It might sound like its easy to change the way you think, but the truth is, it takes a lot of effort on your side to alter your thoughts at least in the immediate future. But never for a second doubt that you can't. Anything that you put your mind to work on, it can be done.

We often limit ourselves due to our beliefs and our thoughts and to the life we know. So the need to be open-minded is an integral part of positive thinking. The bigger we dare to think, the higher and great our changes, possibilities and opportunities. Limitations are created within our minds, and it is up to use to rise above all these obstacles.

Of course, it takes time to change the way we think and see things and broaden our horizons, but small demonstrations of changing our minds and the way we think will yield bigger results in due time.

- **Guidelines for Creating Visualization**

Concise Guidelines for Creative Visualization:

Step 1: Define your goal.

Step 2: Think, meditate and listen to your instinct, ensure that this is the goal you want to attain

Step 3: Ascertain that you only want good results from your visualization, for you and for others around you.

Step 4: Be alone at a place that you will not be disturbed. Be alone with your thoughts.

Step 5: Relax your body and your mind

Step 6: Rhythmically breathe deeply several

Step 7: Visualize your goal by giving it a clear and detailed mental image

Step 8: Add desire and feelings into this mental image- how you would feel etc

Step 9: Use all your five senses of sight, hearing, touch, taste and smell

Step 10: Visualize this at least twice a day for at least 10 minutes each time

Step 11: Keep visualizing this day after day with patience, hope and faith

Step 12: Always keep staying positive in your feelings, thoughts and words

Staying positive can be easy, it is all about training your mind. When you do feel doubts, and negative thoughts arise, replace them with positive thoughts. Also remember to keep an open mind because opportunities come in various ways so when you see it, you can take advantage of them. Every morning, or each time you conclude your visualization session, always end it with this 'Let everything happen in a favorable way for everyone and everything involved.'

Creative visualization will open doors but it takes time and whenever you feel you are in a position of advantage, take action. Do not be passive or wait for things to fall on your lap. Perhaps you've met someone who can put yours in a position of advantage to reach your goal or perhaps you've landed a job that has the possibility of enabling you to travel. All these things come into your life, and if you have an open mind, you can see the possibilities more vividly.

When you use the power of imagination for you and the people around you, always do it for good. Never try creative visualization to obtain something forcibly that belongs to others (like someone else's husband or wife or a managerial position someone else rightfully achieved but you want as well). Also, don't harm the environment.

Most visualized goals happen in a natural and gradual manner, but there can be times that can happen in a sudden and expected manner too. Be realistic with your goals, though. Don't visualize a unicorn and expect it to turn up. If money is what you desire, you know that it just will not drop from the sky. You may or may not win it in the lottery. But the chances or possibilities are higher when you go through life with a new job, or you get a promotion, or you end up making a business deal.

It is always better to think and visualize what you actually want because you do not want to attract situations that are negative, in your quest to fulfill your goals and desires.

Using Affirmations

Affirmations have helped many people make significant changes in their lives and the people around them. Do they work for everyone? Why do some people have achieved success using this technique but some people do not get anything from it?

• What are Affirmations?

Affirmations are positive and direct statements that help an individual overcome self-sabotaging and negative thoughts. It helps a person visualize and believe in their goals, dreams, and abilities. In other words, you are affirming to yourself and helping yourself make positive changes to your life goals. Affirmations have the power to work because it can program a person's mind into believing a concept. The mind is known not to know the difference between what is real or fantasy. That is why when you watch a movie; you tend to empathize with the characters on the screen even though you know it's just a movie. But as soon as you leave the cinema, you are back into reality but can't help feel sorry or happy for the characters.

There are both positive and negative affirmations and some of these affirmations such as being told you are smart when you were a child or being told that you are clumsy can stick with us in both our conscious or unconscious mind. When we face failure, we tend to over-calculate the risks we are taking and work out the worst possible scenario which is usually the emotional equivalent of our parents or guardian deserting us.

We imagine an entirely dreadful scenario in our minds that we convince ourselves that trying to change isn't a good thing at all. Thus, it makes us lose out on opportunities for success and then when we actually do fail (because our mind is already convinced we'll fail anyway) the whole experience of affirmation that we give ourselves is that we are not cut out for success, or it is not in our karma to succeed, and then, we settle.

If a negative belief is firmly rooted in our subconscious mind, then it will have the ability to override any positive affirmation even when we aren't aware of it.

This is one of the reasons why people do not believe in positive affirmations because it doesn't seem to be working. Their negative patterns are so high it just knocks out the sun!

So how do we add affirmations into our daily life and how can we make them prevail above our negative thinking? Here are some steps to follow:

Making Affirmations Work for You

Step 1- On a day that you are alone and not busy or distracted (if you don't have a time like this, then make one) list down all your negative qualities. Include any criticism that others have made of you and those that you have been holding onto. Remember that we all have flaws so do not judge. By acknowledging your mistakes, you can then move forward and work on your flaws, and you can make a shift in your life. When you write these down, take note to see if you are holding any grudges along the way or holding on to it. For example, do you feel tightness or dread in your heart?

Step 2- Begin to write out an affirmation on the positive aspect of your self-assessment. Use powerful statement words to beef up this assessment. Instead of saying 'I am worthy' say 'I am extremely cherished and remarkable.'

Step 3- Practice every day reading this affirmation loudly for five minutes at least three times a day in the morning, afternoon and at night before going to sleep. You can do this while shaving or putting your make up on, or when you are fixing yourself a cup of tea or if you are in the shower. At best, look in the mirror, so you look at yourself and repeat these positive statements. You can also write these affirmations in your notebook at any time you feel like it. Take note of how your writing changes over time. If we do not like something, often writing this down will encompass using smaller handwriting but if we right in big and bold letterings, we are increasing the affirmation of this. This is really a mindfulness journey to get to the agenda of positive affirmation.

Step 4- To enhance the impact, do body movements such as placing your hand on your heart when you felt uncomfortable writing out a negative criticism of yourself in Step 1. As you work on reprogramming your mind to alter it from the concept of affirmation to a real and definite personification of the quality that you see.

Step 5- Get someone to help you repeat your affirmations. This can be a friend or a gym coach or just about anyone that you feel safe with. For example, if they are saying that you are cherished and remarkable, and then connect this statement with your situations such as 'excellent colleague' or 'good fathering.' If you are not comfortable with doing this with someone, then look at your reflection in the mirror and reinforce your positive message.

Affirmations can be an incredibly powerful tool that can help you change your state of mind, alleviate your mood and more importantly, ingrain the changes your desire into your life. But for all of this to happen, you first need to identify the negative and the work on getting rid of them in your life.

Examples of Positive Affirmation
Here are some examples of positive affirmations that you can use to relate to the various areas of your development:

- I know, accept and am true to myself
- I believe in myself and have confidence in my decisions
- I eat a balanced diet, exercise regularly and get plenty of rest
- I always learn from my mistakes
- I know I am capable of anything and can accomplish anything I set my mind to
- I have flaws and I am not perfect but that's ok because I am human
- I never, ever give up

- I can adapt and accept what I have no control over

- I make the best of every situation

- I always look at the bright side of life

- I enjoy life to the fullest

- I stand up for what I believe in, my morals and my values

- I treat others with respect and recognize their individuality

- I can make a difference

- I can practice understanding, patience and compassions

- I am always up to learn new things and be open-minded

- I live in the moment and learn from my past and prepare for my future

These are just some of the positive affirmations that you can use to be optimistic and pursue a fulfilling and happy mindset. Have fun in creating your own affirmations or tailor the above to suit your needs and situation. Most of the affirmations above can be used daily to uplift, inspire and motivate you and those around you.

Mindfulness Meditation for Self-Compassion

Have you thought about meditation or have you done meditation before? Meditation does wonders to your body, mind and soul. When it comes to practising self-compassion, mindful meditation helps you incorporate this into your daily life more frequently. Keep in mind that mindful meditation isn't only helpful for self-compassion but it also helps us deal with the negativity that we face when we want to practice self-compassion.

Exercise 1 – Mindful Breathing

Breathing is an essential part of the meditative experience, so it is only natural that we should

exercise this too. Whenever you meditate, you're breathing mindfully when you focus on each purposeful breath that goes in and out of your body. Mindful breathing doesn't just have to happen when you're meditating, it can be done anywhere and at any time whether you're sitting, standing or just walking about. Make it a habit to breathe mindfully and you'll find it much easier to do so during your meditation sessions.

1. Start by bringing your attention and focus to your breathing.
2. Breathe in slowly for approximately 3 seconds, and then release that breathe slowly, counting to 3 seconds again.
3. During this exercise, you should focus and be thinking of nothing else except your breathing. Do not think about the tasks you need to do, or a meeting that is coming up at work. Think about nothing but your breathing in and out, counting the seconds as you do.
4. Concentrate on the air that is filling your lungs as you breathe in, the way it makes your body feel, and when you release your breathe, imagine all the stress and the tension leaving your body as you do.

You can do this for 1-2 minutes at a time throughout the day, several times a day and you're already on your way towards improving each meditation session when you get better at learning to control your breathing.

Exercise 2 – Awareness

When you meditate, you learn to become more aware of your body, your mind and your thoughts, aware of what is happening all around you when your eyes are closed because your other senses become heightened when your eyes are shut. Being mindfully aware helps you sharpen your focus and remain alert to not just your surroundings, but your thoughts as well. For example, if you were mindfully aware about your thoughts, you will have better control when it comes to keeping any negative thought or emotion at bay.

Exercising your awareness throughout the day will help sharpen your alertness towards everything around you. Not just around you, but within you too. Beginners often find focusing on awareness to be a struggle in the beginning, because its so easy to let our thoughts drift and get distracted by everything else. Training yourself to be more aware will help you better connect your mind and body during your meditation sessions, so it's a good idea to practice these throughout the day to help you sharpen your focus and cultivate a heightened sense of awareness.

1. Start by choosing an activity or an object to focus on. Pick something that you would normally do without thinking twice about it, like opening the door or getting dressed in the morning for example.

2. Once you've got your object or activity, start to really, actively pay attention to what you're doing. If you're opening the door, concentrate on it. Reach for the doorknob and be aware of how it feels in your hand, and the motion of pulling the door towards you or away from you. Stop and appreciate how lucky you are to be healthy and fit enough to walk out your front door with a destination and a purpose in mind.

3. When you're getting dressed in the morning, focus and be aware of what you're doing instead of just going through the motions. Concentrate on how the fabric of your clothes feel in your hand, and even stop to appreciate how fortunate you are to be able to have a selection of clothes to choose from as you go through your closet looking for something to wear.

4. Before you eat, be aware of the food that is in front of you, how good it smells, the shapes, the colors. As you take each bite and begin to chew, be aware of how the food tastes and you take each bite with purpose.

Eventually, being mindfully aware is something that will come much easier, and the more you practice the easier you will find it is to concentrate on what you're doing or thinking without becoming easily distracted by other thoughts around you.

Exercise 3 – Mental Focus

Successful meditation involves being able to concentrate and not let your thoughts get easily distracted, which means you're going to need to work on improving your focus. Exercises to improve your focus are simple enough, here's what you can do:

1. Pick an object to focus on and place it in front of you.
2. When you're ready, set a timer and start to focus on the object and nothing else.
3. Concentrate on that object and keep staring at it for as long as you can.
4. When your mind begins to wander, stop and make a note of how long you managed to concentrate on that object before your mind started to drift.
5. Next round, do the same thing but try to go for a longer time this time around, aiming to beat your previous record.

Gradually, you should be able to focus on the object in front of you for longer periods of time before you find yourself getting distracted. The longer you can focus on the object, the better your focusing abilities will become.

PART III

PART III

Chapter 1: Why So Sensitive?

"For a highly sensitive person, a drizzle feels like a monsoon."

-Anonymous

When something out of the ordinary happens, and it is relatively minor, you may become a little surprised, sad, anxious, or happy, depending on what the situation is. Even though the event happened out of nowhere, it elicits a minor emotional response. This will be the case if your emotional reactions are that of a normal individual. However, if you are part of the subset of the population which is highly sensitive, then your response will be anything but minor.

Imagine going completely over the top with your feelings when something out of the ordinary happens in your life. If you go through a distraught situation, you become much more saddened than those around you. If a friend has something good happen to them, you will act more excited than they do. When someone is loud, you feel it to your core. If this sounds like you, then you might be a highly sensitive person.

Individuals who are highly sensitive display stronger reactivity to external and internal stimuli, whether emotional, physical, or social. They are thought to have deeper sensitivities at the central nervous system. It is estimated that about 15-20 percent of the population falls under this umbrella. Highly sensitive persons are believed to be much more disturbed by violence or tension. If they see something bad happen on the news, they will be distraught and might even be bothered by it the whole day. In contrast, someone who is not in their shoes will just think about it for a moment. On the flip side, if you make them happy, they will be exceptionally excited beyond control. It's how they are built.

This may not sound like a big deal to most. You have probably known several people who are overly emotional. However, this goes beyond just crying a little extra during a movie. If you were to go inside the mind of a highly sensitive person, what you are likely to experience would overwhelm you instantly. If you are living with this mindset, then you know exactly what I am talking about.

Despite what people may think, highly sensitive people are not dramatic for no reason. They often cannot help the way they react in certain situations. At least, not without becoming aware of it first. These individuals will often notice things much more acutely than other people do. This relates especially to the feelings of others. While most individuals will simply overlook the pain and suffering of someone else, a highly sensitive person will be more aware of their emotions. They may not know exactly what is wrong, but just that something is okay. They will pick up on the subtleties of body language, facial expressions, and tone of voice. Even if they don't know an individual, they will be in-tune with the vibes the person puts off. All sensitivity radars will be off the charts.

How To Tell If You're In The Camp

If you have always felt a little different than everybody else around you, then you might be dealing with a highly sensitive personality. Of course, there are many different attributes to consider before knowing for sure. The following are some of the signs of being in this camp. Once you understand whether you're a highly sensitive person or not, then we can proceed forward.

- You are extremely unsettled by cruelty or violence. While most people don't enjoy violence, a highly sensitive person will become extremely disturbed or physically ill by it, even if they don't see it personally.

- You are frequently emotionally exhausted because of how others feel. Essentially, other people and their feelings have a deep impact on you.

- Time crunches make you extremely anxious and overwhelmed. While approaching deadlines can make anyone's hair get raised, it is exponentially greater for a highly sensitive person.

- You enjoy going int solitude at the end of the day to reduce your stimulation levels.

- You are very jumpy and become frightened quickly.

- You are a very deep thinker. You often reflect on your life and experiences to process everything. You will also play events in your head over and over again.

- You seek to find answers to life's questions and wonder why things are the way they are.

- You are startled easily by sudden, loud noises.

- You have reduced pain tolerance.

- You have a rich inner world. You probably grew up with many imaginary friends and might still have them as an adult. You frequently go into a fantasy world.

- You are extremely upset by change, whether positive or negative. It can really throw you off.

- You are very sensitive to the environmental stimuli around you, like the birds chirping, sirens, new smells, or unusual sites. This is because all of your senses are heightened.

- When you're hungry, you become angry too.

- You hate conflict and disagreements. You want people to get along and not fight with each other. You definitely avoid confrontation if you can.

- You are very thin-skinned. You do not take criticism well, whether it is constructive or not.

- You're very conscientious of making mistakes. You're not perfect, but you try extremely hard to be.

- The beauty of your surroundings moves you deeply. Whether it is artwork, a rich scent, or a delicious looking meal, you are enthralled by all of it.

- You will compare yourself to others and often feel inferior as a result.

- You are very perceptive and insightful. You pick up on things that others don't.

If you have been dealing with the issue of being highly sensitive, then you have probably been looked down upon your whole life. People may have told you to toughen up, be less sensitive, or grow a backbone. Don't take any of these statements personally because these individuals did not know better. In fact, you may not have known better and thought there was something wrong with you. Well, as you read further, you will actually begin to understand your unique gifts.

What Makes People Overly Sensitive?

There are many factors to consider when deciding on why you are a highly sensitive person. If having these feelings is an anomaly for you, meaning it's not your normal personality, then it is probably a unique life event that is causing you to behave in this manner. For example, losing a loved one, having poor health, not eating properly, or getting a lack of sleep may contribute to feelings of over sensitivity. However, if you have always been this way, then it goes well-beyond life events. It is ingrained in you to be a highly sensitive person.

Children who were severely criticized, bullied, or went through some type of abuse or trauma can also end up being highly sensitive. Their psyches took a major hit while they were children, so they grew up to be unsure of themselves, which may have contributed to their over-sensitivity, as a result.

Your highly sensitive feelings are likely to have a genetic component to them. So, you might have been born this way as it was passed on through your genes. Also, environmental and social factors may be involved. If your parents, or those you grew up around, were highly sensitive people, then you might have picked up on their personality traits and acquired them as your own. Of course, you can also end up completely opposite from your parents and other influential people, so their attributes may not mean anything in relation to you.

Overall, a highly sensitive person is thought to have a brain that is wired differently, so it has a lower threshold for the environment. So, any type of stimulus will have an exponential effect on them. Many of these characteristics can be seen in babies, as some infants are much more emotional and sensitive to things like sound. This further suggests that people are born highly sensitive, rather than made. In the mid-1990s, husband and wife psychology duo, Arthur and Elaine Aron, coined the term "sensory-processing sensitivity," which is the official scientific phrase used to describe a highly sensitive person. Through their research, the husband and wife duo stated further that the nervous system of someone with sensory-processing sensitivity had variations in their nervous system that was different from others who did not display highly sensitive qualities.

Negative Aspects Of Being A Highly Sensitive Person

Being in the camp of high sensitivity can certainly have their advantages, which we will go over in the next chapter. For now, I will discuss the negative aspects of being a highly sensitive person. This personality trait can impact every area of your life, and if you are not careful, it can create a lot of pain and suffering in the long run. Unfortunately, people will take advantage of the kind qualities of a sensitive individual, and the results are not always pleasant.

In The Workplace

If you are like the majority of people in the world, then you probably spend much of your time in the workplace. Here, you will have regular interactions with your coworkers and those in upper management. While certain things in the workplace may be a slight struggle or annoyance for most individuals, a highly sensitive person may have their whole workflow and mood affected in a significant way. The following are certain obstacles that only a highly sensitive person would understand and contend within the workplace.

- A strong aroma in the office can completely throw off a highly sensitive person. These can be smells that come from different foods or from someone wearing a lot of perfume.

- Other sensory issues like bright colors or loud sounds in the workspace, can severely affect their focus and ability to do their job.

- Trying to complete last-minute deadlines without proper planning can cause a highly sensitive person to become overwhelmed quickly. This is definitely not when they do their best work.

- Criticism from a boss or employee can truly mess with a highly sensitive person's head. They may even react in an unorthodox fashion, like having a mental breakdown, crying excessively, or running out of the office. They often cannot help it as it is an instantaneous reaction.

- Highly sensitive people will have a hard time speaking up and asking for what they want or need. They hate rocking the boat and definitely don't want to upset anyone else. As a result, they are often overlooked for many opportunities.

- These individuals are often seen as weak and ineffectual, so people will walk all over them. The highly sensitive person will usually let them.

- They are usually overstressed, even if it's a normal workday with nothing unusual going on. Anything in their environment can make them feel this way. Remember that highly sensitive people are more prone to be affected by environmental stimuli.

- There will be constant comparison with coworkers, and the highly sensitive person will always feel like they come up short.

- Wearing professional clothes, like ties, high-heels, or various other things that are uncomfortable, are highly bothersome to you.

As a highly sensitive person, you must be aware of these unique traits and how they will make you react. Otherwise, your experience at work will become constant suffrage.

In Their Personal Lives

Highly sensitive people will also deal with others in their personal lives, both at home and in various relationships. Their personality traits will often not do them any favors in this aspect of their lives, either. As a highly sensitive person, you will have extremely emotional and sometimes hostile relationships with those close to you. The following are some issues you may run into.

- Highly sensitive people will sense when their friends and family are going through some issues. They will also allow these emotions to overwhelm them.

- If a highly sensitive person gets asked to do something, in most cases, they will say yes, no matter how busy their schedule is or what they have planned. Saying no is a true challenge.

- These individuals are their own worst critic and will be excessively hard on themselves for something, while easily forgiving someone else for the same issues.

- They are often poor with self-care because they are too busy worrying about others.

- They are more sensitive to trouble and conflict within a relationship. They will become stressed easily during a conflict.

- They will have a lot of self-doubt about their abilities, which will show in their personal relationships. They will usually be the ones to submit and compromise full.

- They will have a hard time asking their friends for anything.

- It will be very easy to hurt a highly sensitive person's feelings. Plus, they can be manipulated easily.

As you can see, a highly sensitive person will not have an easy time with their personal relationships. They will usually be the givers and never the takers. These qualities can wear down on them and create much emotional and psychological harm if not dealt with accordingly.

Now that we have a picture of what a highly sensitive person is, you probably have a pretty good idea if you are one or not. We will get into more detail about the positive qualities of this personality trait.

Chapter 2: Embrace Your Sensitivities

I know I was pretty hard on highly sensitive people in chapter one and did not paint them in the most positive light. It is hard to imagine that these individuals actually have positive qualities. However, just because a highly sensitive person has flaws and weaknesses does not mean they don't have significant strengths too. In this section, I will go over the reasons why being a highly sensitive person is a good thing and how people can start embracing this aspect of themselves.

Benefits Of Being a Highly Sensitive Person

There are actually many great qualities to being a highly sensitive person, and the world is lucky to have individuals like this. Sensitivity is falsely depicted as being undesirable, which you have probably noticed in your own life. I am here to tell you that it is not a negative trait to have. With all of the controversy surrounding it, the benefits are often overlooked. But, they cannot be ignored any longer.

Having A Depth Of Experience And Feelings

Experiencing the world with heightened emotions gives you a deeper meaning in everything around you. You learn to find joy in the smallest things, which means you have the ability to find good in every area of life. You learn to experience life in a totally different way as a highly sensitive person and notice beauty in the subtleties of life.

Self-Awareness

Self-awareness means having a strong sense of who you are and where you belong in the world. A highly sensitive person has a keen self-awareness. They are hyper tuned in to their emotions, and the reactions that follow them. While a highly sensitive person understands their high levels of emotional volatility, they eventually realize that other people do not process feelings in the same manner that they do. What throws their minds for a loop, will barely be a blip on the radar for someone else.

Intuitive Nurturing Skills

The highly sensitive person is naturally good at nurturing others. Because of their ability to feel deeply, they have a strong desire to bring happiness to other people. They have the instinct to care for others and will support them, so they feel loved and appreciated.

A Knack For Forming Close relationships

Highly sensitive people may take a while to open up to somebody, but once they do, they form strong bonds in the process. They will become the best companions a person can have. The reason highly sensitive people are choosy with making friends is because they can feel the energy of others around them. If the energies don't mesh, they know the relationships won't be a good fit.

Highly sensitive people are not interested in casual acquaintances, but in developing meaningful relationships. They want to be around individuals who make them feel comfortable.

Appreciating The Small Things In Life

Highly sensitive people are also highly sensitive to things that bring them joy. This means they can find joy in even the smallest things in life. If they are having a bad day, hearing a good song on the radio can completely change their mood.

Why Highly Sensitive People Make Great Friends

As we move through life, we meet and develop relationships with many different people. While we get along and also get to know these individuals well, how many of them truly become great friends? It is rare to find friends who understand us for who we are, leave us feeling warm and make us believe that we are important. A highly sensitive person is a friend who has all of these abilities. These individuals become the best kinds of friends because of the attributes they possess. The following are a few reasons why a highly sensitive person should be a sought-after relationship in your life.

- They are able to manage conflicts well because they have the ability to observe and quickly diffuse a situation. Plus, they have a keen eye for details and can often sense a conflict erupting before it starts.
- They highly understand the needs of others and will work hard to keep their friends happy, including you.
- They like to involve others and help them grow. Even when you make a mistake, they will help you learn from it and maintain your confidence.
- They are not stuck in their own worlds.
- They have a sense of purpose and want to make a difference in people's lives.

If you are a highly sensitive person, know that you can be a great and valuable friend to many people out there.

Why Highly Sensitive People Make Great Employees

While highly sensitive people can struggle in major ways in many work environments, they actually make great employees. The attributes they have make them reliable, hardworking, intuitive, and great team players. Rarely will they cause drama. In fact, they will do their best to avoid it.

Highly sensitive people are often undervalued in the workplace. They are not the most charismatic or outspoken people in the office. In fact, they are probably the ones you will hear from the least. Unfortunately, the soft skills they bring to the table do not get the same recognition as the stronger skills. This does not mean they are less valuable as employees, though. The following are some of the reasons highly sensitive people are a great addition to any company.

- They are the ones you can count on. They have the right attitude, will always show up, and will put in the effort needed to get the job done.
- They are careful decision-makers and will rarely take action hastily. As a result, the decisions they make are often the best possible under the circumstances at the moment.
- If they are in a positive environment, they will thrive beyond your imagination.
- They can be creative and, therefore, find the right solutions to problems.
- People often think that leaders have to be loud and brash. Actually, this is the opposite of what a leader should be. True leaders are intuitive, listen well, and inspire others. This is why a highly sensitive person actually makes a great leader.
- Highly sensitive people will focus on what benefits the team, rather than what benefits themselves.

If you are a highly sensitive person, know that your attributes are truly desired in the workplace, even if it doesn't seem that way.

Guess what? As a highly sensitive person, you are special and bring a unique gift to this world. Too many people are stuck in their own heads and have no concept or understanding of the world around them. You, on the other hand, can acknowledge the thoughts and feelings of other people. Because of your great attributes, you must stop believing that you are undesirable or weak. You are actually the strong one. The next chapter will discuss how you can start believing in yourself and the value that you bring to the world. You will become a better person overall.

Chapter 3: Living As A Highly Sensitive Person

The key to living a happy life as a highly sensitive person is to embrace the good qualities that you possess and showcase them to the world, while not allowing your flaws to control you. The bad part about highly sensitive people is that their oversensitivity gets the best of them, and often at the most inopportune times. The goal of this chapter will be to focus on controlling your emotions and allowing your unique gifts to shine through by using specific action steps to rewire your brain and way of thinking. Mindset shifts will be a major factor in managing your habits and sensitivities. Once you go through the practices and action steps I discuss here; you will truly be able to live your best life as a highly sensitive person.

The first step in the process is realizing who you are. In the previous two chapters, I detailed the positive and negative attributes of a highly sensitive person. In the end, while having this trait has extreme downsides, the positives outweigh the negatives. If you have come to realize that you are a highly sensitive person, then it's time to move on to the strategies and actions steps to manage your emotions.

How To Overcome Your Sensitivities

Just to be clear, you will never get rid of your sensitivities. They have always been a part of who and always will be. The objective is to manage these sensitivities, so you can overcome them. If they control you, they can become a major obstacle. The key is to use them to your advantage by controlling them. The following are some survival tips for highly sensitive people so that they don't become overwhelmed.

- Get plenty of sleep. Usually, 7-8 hours is recommended, but whatever it takes t make you feel well-rested. A lack of sleep will make you irritable, moody, less productive, and decrease your concentration. Proper sleep will help soothe your senses.

- Eat healthy food throughout the day. People dismiss how much of an effect diet has on your mood. But, if you eat foods high in cholesterol, saturated fats, and sugars, you will become tired, irritable, and overly sensitive to stimuli.

- A good pair of headphones can keep you from getting triggered with loud noises. You cannot control the noise, but you can manage how much it affects you.

- Plan time to decompress. Being on the go all the time will always keep you on heightened alert. This means you will continuously be in a frazzled state of mind. Taking time to decompress, preferably at night, can allow your nerves to calm down and no longer be affected by external stimuli. Whatever you can do to isolate yourself from the craziness of the world, do it.

- Give yourself the time and space to get things done. Highly sensitive people do not do well with a packed schedule, so avoid getting yourself in this position if you can help it.

- Limit your caffeine intake. Caffeine is a natural stimulant that will make you feel jittery if taken in excess. Highly sensitive people might be even more sensitive to caffeine. If you drink two cups of coffee a day, cut it down to one.

- Try to avoid excessively lighted areas if you can. In your home, keep your lights dim, as well.

- Get your errands done during the off-hours. This means going out opposite the average person's regular schedule. Get your shopping done during the week, go out with friends on weeknights, and go to the gym early in the morning. The goal here is to avoid huge crowds that can stir up your emotions.

- Get out in nature as much as possible and get away from the hustle-and-bustle of the city.

Even though you are born being highly sensitive, there are still many environmental factors that can trigger you to become more over the top. The survival tips above are meant to prevent overloading your hypersensitive senses. Many psychologists and research scientists have stated that a proper lifestyle may not change our genetics, but it can keep it from making our issues worse.

Having Self-Esteem As A Highly Sensitive Person

Te thing that highly sensitive people struggle with the most is their self-esteem, which is the value and worth they place on themselves. This is because they allow their environment, including the people, around them, to dictate their emotions. It is difficult for these individuals to break away from the feeling other people are having. As a highly sensitive person yourself, it's time for you to start realizing the importance of self-esteem and begin to recognize ways you can improve your own. It is time to stop thinking you are not good enough. The following strategies will take a lot of practice, but once you start implementing them, you will notice major changes in your mindset.

Accept Thoughts, Emotions, And Sensations As They Are

All of these aspects are a part of you but do not define you. They are fleeting in nature and are changing from moment to moment. If you are feeling pain, whether emotional or physical, for a definitive moment, that does not mean you are weak. It is a sensation you are going through that will eventually pass. Instead of letting your thoughts and feeling control you, work on observing them objectively and then letting them go. Do not allow them to become attached to you.

Eliminate The Word "Should" From Your Vocabulary

When you use the word "should," it will elicit a sense of guilt inside of you. If you change it to "could," then you subconsciously open up your mind about what you could be doing and uses less judgment. Using the word "could" also showcases that there are many different options for us, and we are not required to stay on one path. Try it out:

"I should be going to the gym." Change it to, "I could be going to the gym." See the difference?

Do Not Rely On Other People For Self-Esteem

Unfortunately, as highly sensitive people, most of our self-worth is dependent on what other people think of us. You will never place true value on yourself if this is the mindset you will carry. The major problem is that when our outside source for self-esteem vanishes, then the opinion we have of ourselves plummets. We have to internalize our power to create our value and become the sole person who is in charge of it.

Forgive

We all have something in our past that we are not proud of. We must learn to forgive ourselves for the mistakes we made so we can move on. We need to apply the same compassion for ourselves that we tend to show other people. The next time you are hard on yourself, imagine one of your best friends standing in your position. Now, picture what you would tell this person if they made the same mistakes you did. If it's something favorable, then tell yourself the same thing. Stop being your worst critic.

Take Stock Of Your Talents

We tend to focus on our faults, and this severely lowers our self-esteem. We do not give ourselves enough credit by doing this. It is time to take stock of your talents and remember the gifts that you bring to the world. Identify what you are good at. If you are having a tough time coming up with something, then start small. Perhaps you are good at putting things away. This is a good start. As you come up with things, write them down and keep them to look at constantly. Another exercise you can do is write down what you think you're not good at and then crumble up that piece of paper and throw it away. Focus on your positive attributes.

Remember that these exercises will take a lot of consistency. Do not just quit after one day. When you begin incorporating these strategies into your daily life, you will see vast improvements with your mindset.

Focusing On Jobs, You Are Good At

I discussed in the previous chapter about highly sensitive people being model employees. This is still true. However, the goal is to make yourself as happy as possible, and this means avoiding things that will trigger your sensitivities. That being said, there are certain environments and job types where a highly sensitive person will fit in better and even thrive. If you can avoid the stress altogether, then why not do so? The following are the best career options for you if you are a highly sensitive person.

Caring Professions

Careers that require a lot of caring and compassion will be right up a highly sensitive person's alley. These jobs include things like nursing, medicine, counseling, therapy, and coaching. These fields will target a highly sensitive person's strength. Bear in mind that certain areas, like the emergency department or the ICU, may be challenging areas for you. Also, any busy environment will have a lot of different emotions that you will have to contend with. Good options in these fields may be things like home health nursing or individual counseling.

Creative Endeavors

Highly sensitive people are often very creative, so they will thrive in professions where they can show off their creativity. Some of these roles include graphic designer, writer, photographer, artist, or architect. Many creative jobs can be done on a freelance basis, which allows you to create your own schedule. This will be a major benefit to you as a highly sensitive person.

Clergy

If you have a spiritual side to you, then working as a clergy person may be right for you. Bear in mind, that depending on the denomination, you may have to follow strict rules. This may cause difficulty if you are a highly open-minded person. Of course, if you can get over the structure, then your intuition and sensitivity will be valued and accepted.

Academia

With academia, you get to spend a significant amount of time doing thoughtful and intensive research on a subject you have an interest in. In addition, you get to teach your extensive knowledge to students; as a highly sensitive person, you will thrive in your areas. In the end, you are doing meaningful work throughout your profession.

IT Professional

Coding is a major portion of IT and requires a lot of creativity to be successful. You will also need strong intuition and an eye for detail. These are all qualities that are possessed by highly sensitive people. As one of these individuals, software engineering or website development might be the perfect career paths for you.

When choosing a career to go into, you should focus on your strengths and what areas you will be compatible with. Consider your strengths as a highly sensitive person and determine what line of work fits you best.

Dealing With Hyperarousal

There will be times when you are in a state of hyperarousal, where you will be wired up and out of control, physically and mentally. In some cases, hyperarousal can be a defense mechanism, like with the fight-or-flight response. In these moments, being on high alert is a necessity. However, when the hyperarousal goes beyond defined moments, you will be dealing with many problems, including stress, anxiety, and overall diminished emotional and physical health. Yes, being in a state of constant arousal is detrimental to your physical health. Prolonged stress has led to many chronic illnesses, like heart disease, stroke, diabetes, and even some cancers. In addition, mental health disorders like depression are also a possibility.

When you are in the hyperarousal state, you will have an increased heart rate, faster breathing, quicker reflexes, perspiration, and heightened sensitivity to stimuli. So, when you hear a loud noise, you will immediately jump into action, or at least be ready to. Once again, short-term physiological responses like these are not dangerous. If you are consistently in this state, then we have a problem that must be addressed.

Hyperarousal needs to be dealt with quickly; otherwise, it will take over your life. This response is a symptom of another problem, so if you can figure out that problem is, then you can address it directly. The following are some action steps that will have a favorable response to being wired.

Practice Mindfulness

The purpose of this technique is to sit peacefully and consciously observe the chaos and frantic thoughts going on inside your mind without trying to change them, escape from them, or fight them off. Many therapists use this technique with their clients because it is effective in getting over feelings of panic. It also helps to reduce your hyperarousal symptoms.

Perform this technique for about 1-5 minutes at a time. Just sit quietly and focus on your feelings of discomfort, agitation, and anxiety. Concentrate very hard in this area. See if you can visualize these negative feelings and imagine holding them in your arms. A common practice that therapists have their clients do is picture the problems they are holding as being much bigger and worse. It may sound confusing, but it works well for their clients. It is likely because once they've imagined the issue being worse, the thing does not seem as major.

Make Small Achievable Goals Towards Relaxation And Calmness

I do mean to make these goals achievable by keeping them small. When you first start out, shoot for 30 seconds of pure relaxations. Once you achieve this milestone, then try for one minute, then two minutes, and so on. Eventually, you will be able to be in this state for several minutes with no problems. Just work your way up.

It does not matter what relaxation techniques you use, as long as you are in a state of physical relaxation and calmness. This can mean lying down in bed, sitting in a comfortable chair, or meditating. The choice is yours. From here, remain quiet and focus on a body part that feels tense. Now, take one breath in slowly over a few seconds, then hold it for a few seconds before letting it out slowly. As you release the breath, imagine the tension leaving that part of the body you focused on earlier. Truly visualize the tension dissipating like a cloud of smoke.

Evaluate yourself after this. Did your breathing and pulse rate decrease? Do you feel less tense and anxious? If so, then the practice was a success. Keep working on this step to make yourself better.

Positive Self-Talk

In the middle of frantic self-talk that is negative, interrupt yourself and begin saying some encouraging phrases. These include statements like, "You will get through this," or "You are strong and will overcome." This technique will trick your mind and shift it from positive to negative. As a result, you will slow down your pace. Once you do this often, it will become a habit.

Investigate The Root Cause

The above exercises are beneficial; however, you should also determine what the root cause of your hyperarousal is. If you can figure this out, then the risk of flareups in the future will go down. Some of the causes include anxiety, PTSD, excess caffeine, and drug or alcohol use. Once you've narrowed it down, then you can focus on more specific techniques to eliminate the root cause.

For example, Cognitive Behavioral Therapy, or CBT, can be an effective strategy from anxiety. The goal of CBT is to challenge your current thought patterns through talk therapy. The following are a few key steps to make CBT work for you.

- Identify what you are thinking by actually writing them down on something. This way, you can visualize them.
- Assess your thoughts and realize that they may not be true or accurate. We often think negative thoughts for so long that we automatically assume they identify us, and we never challenge them.
- Replace these harmful thoughts with more positive and encouraging ones. Write down all of these new thoughts, as well.
- Now, read these new thoughts to yourself over and over again. Do this until it becomes a habit for you to think of these thoughts, which could take days or weeks.

CBT is a strategy that works for many different disorders, and therapists use it often.

The bottom line to all of this is that you will always be a highly sensitive person. It is not something you can avoid, nor should you try to do so. Despite the challenges that may exist, being a highly sensitive person is still a unique gift that you should embrace every day. Learning the techniques to control your thoughts and emotions, and not allowing your environment to overwhelm, you will ensure that you live a happy and satisfying life. Your sensitivity and intuitiveness are a true gift for many people.

PART IV

Chapter 1: What is Holding You Back

The first half of this book focused on the negative aspects of clutter and how removing unnecessary items from your life can be cathartic in so many ways. The goal of all of this was to begin getting things done in your life. This includes all aspects of a person's personal and professional life. Honestly, decluttering was just the first step. It was a way to clear up our minds and reduce distractions. After doing this, it is time to start moving forward and getting things done in our lives. Now that our physical and mental spaces are clear, what else can we focus on? The goal of this chapter is to present some of the biggest challenges to getting things done.

Why People Procrastinate

Procrastination is something many people in our society suffer with. It is the purposeful and unnecessary delay of actions or decisions. Why do something now when you can just do it tomorrow? Well, because you never know what tomorrow will bring. Other challenges will arise, distractions will come up, and you will continue to load up your plate because you refuse to take things off of it. Since you are making the excuse today for waiting until tomorrow, what is stopping you from making the same excuse tomorrow, or the next day and the next day?

Imagine being at a buffet and loading up your plate. When you go to sit down, you decide not to eat much of the food because you want it later. Instead, you go and grab another plate to fill up and bring back to the table. Now, you have two plates to finish, and you have no idea how you will do it. Eventually, the restaurant is about to close, and you don't have the time or space to finish everything. You will most likely waste a large portion of the food. This is what procrastination looks like in life. You keep pushing things back until you become overloaded, overwhelmed, and very close to the deadline, if you even make it at all.

Procrastination is one of the worst enemies of getting things done. It really has no value, except for the fact that some people thrive on making quick deadlines. However, you will also be more likely to make big mistakes. You will never be able to complete the work to your full potential because so many things will be missed. Even if they're minor, they still add up.

Procrastination leads to so many missed opportunities too. Several people do not pursue their goals because they put them off for too long. Eventually, they get to the point where they lose interest or become too involved in other things to where they no longer have time.

People assume that procrastination has everything to do with will power. While this can be a major reason, for sure, it is not the only one that exists. There are many deeper reasons for why people put things off. There are some psychological aspects that are at play. For example, anxiety and fear of failure will terrify people into paralysis. Nobody wants to fail, and if they start something, failure is a huge possibility. As a result, we delay starting anything. At least then, we can save face

124

a little bit.

When our motivation to complete a task outweighs the negative aspects, then there's a strong chance we will still finish it. However, if the negative aspects outweigh our own motivation, then we will put off pursuing a goal if we even do so at all. The following are some other factors that keep up from moving forward. If we follow these, we will always procrastinate.

Abstract Goals

If a person has a vague or abstract goal, then they are more likely to procrastinate. They are not excited enough about it. In fact, they might not even know what the goal is, as there is no clear definition. For example, making a promise to get fit is an abstract goal. It is a simple statement with no real substance. What are the chances you will get fit if you have no actual plan in place for doing so? Furthermore, what does "get fit" even mean to? Does it mean losing a certain amount of weight, gaining muscle, looking slimmer, having more energy, or a combination of all? Honestly, you are not even giving yourself a chance to obtain this goal, as you will just put it off until you forget about it.

A more solid goal would be, "I will lose 15 pounds within two months and be able to run six miles by then." This is a concrete goal with real values and end results. From here, you can create specific action steps to get there. For example, losing two pounds and increasing your run mileage by one every week. Once you create real goals with a legitimate plan, then you are more likely to not put things off.

Not Having Foreseeable Rewards

Many individuals put things off because they see no actual rewards in the near future. For example, a teenager may not attend college because he or she cannot fathom waiting four years or more to get a degree in something that might make them money. In addition, the money will not come right away, which is another deterrent.

People often want immediate pleasure rather than long-term success. This can be seen in people neglecting to create savings or investment accounts. They do not want money later; they want it now. As a result, they delay setting up one of these essential accounts because they can't see the benefits they will create in the future.

This same mindset can apply to punishments, as well. The farther into the future a punishment is, the less likely it will motivate someone to take action. If you are studying for a final exam in college and it is months away, you are not that concerned about it, because even if you fail, it will be a while until that actually happens.

A Disconnect from Our Future Selves

People tend to procrastinate because they cannot comprehend a connection between their present and future selves. They believe the two individuals are mutually exclusive for some reason and don't realize that they are creating their future person by the actions you take today.

A person may delay starting a healthy diet because they cannot see themselves overweight and dealing with chronic diseases in the future. A company someone works for has a chance of going out of business, but the employee does not work on his resume because he cannot see himself being out of work. In both of these examples, their present and future selves are completely different people.

Being Too Optimistic

Now, being optimistic is not a bad thing; however, getting to the point where you overthink your abilities can be a problem. This is a common occurrence as many people do not work on tasks in the present because they highly believe they can complete it in the future. While this may be true, there will still be an increased amount of stress and anxiety. Also, the potential for oversight and significant errors will be present.

Imagine that you have a 10,000-word paper due to Friday, and it is only Monday. It would make sense to write 1,000-2,000 words daily, instead of waiting until Wednesday or Thursday. When writing the paper ahead of time, you will have extra opportunities to think everything through, and also go back and edit your work. Giving yourself extra time will help you in creating quality work.

Being Indecisive

This is when you cannot make a move because you cannot decide what course of action to take. For example, you may hesitate to apply for a job because you cannot decide which one is best for you. This is a phenomenon known as analysis paralysis, and it has stopped many great people right in their tracks. The following are some factors that make it difficult to make a decision.

- The more options you have, the harder it will be to decide a preferable path to take.
- The more similar different options are, the harder it will be to choose. You might end up analyzing the smallest sectors of each choice.
- The more important the decision is, the harder it will be to make because of the impact it will have on you and others.

It is best if you can keep your decisions to a minimum, as well as your choices. Each time you make a decision, you deplete your mental resources to a degree. So, if you make a host of decisions in a short time period, you have a high likelihood of getting burned out.

Task Aversion

People often procrastinate because they are not looking forward to a task they need to perform. For example, they might have to call them back to resolve a payment dispute but are not looking forward to talking with a customer service representative. As a result, They put off doing it. If you are avoiding a task because of the aversion you have to it, you are just delaying your agony. Imagine how good you will feel after doing it. So, hold your nose and get it done.

Perfectionism

People often want things so perfect that they are terrified of doing something out of fear of the mistakes they will make. Instead of starting and taking their chances, they avoid moving forward. Perfectionism has been called the enemy of productivity because of all the delays it creates along the way. People do not realize that things will no be perfect, so they waste excessive time trying to ake things this way.

Self-Handicapping

Many individuals are terrified of exposing their lack of ability for something. As a result, they procrastinate so they can use it as an excuse for poor performance. They would rather that people think they're lazy than incapable. Procrastinators with this mindset are more likely to put things off if they feel that failure will reflect badly on them.

These are some of the most common reasons for procrastination. There is no easy answer to why people avoid doing things, but it must be overcome for people to start accomplishing things. The following are a few more reasons for procrastination:

- Self-sabotage
- Low self-efficacy
- Perceived lack of self-control
- Fear of being criticized

Sometimes, there are more urgent situations, like ADHD, depression, or low self-esteem, that need to be addressed. The better question to ask is: Why put something off until tomorrow if I can get it done today?

Other Major Reasons for Not Getting Things Done

For some reason, people are just not getting as many things done as they could. Now, I am not saying you have to be on the go all the time. That is not healthy, either. What I am saying is that you need to accomplish things within a certain time period, or you will never achieve anything in life. This will not just affect you, but those who rely on you, as well, like employees, business partners, and family members. To make the world go around, people need to get things done. Yet, they don't. I already spoke about procrastination as a major factor. I will now detail a few other reasons why this happens.

Not Sure What to do

Many people do not do anything because they have no idea what they should do. Even if they have a goal, they are clueless about how to get started in any way. This often occurs because we see other people's accomplishments but have no idea how they achieved them. We keep trying to guess but can't figure it out. Even if we do become aware of how something was accomplished, the values do not line up with our own, which makes us even more confused. It is better to keep on track with your own beliefs when trying to accomplish a goal, rather than rejecting them completely. Rejecting your values will make you even more confused.

There is No Deadline or Accountability

Accountability seems to be going by the wayside these days. People don't get things done because they are not expected to. There is often no disciplinary actions taken, so people continue to lack the drive to move forwards.

Also, when deadlines are nonexistent, then there is no need to get moving. Either we don't create deadlines for ourselves, or other people don't place them on us. If you work for someone and they do not set deadlines, then the operations of the company are not very sound. If you do not set your own deadlines for goals, then you need to start doing so. Make them concrete and not too far out. Remember, you don't want to fall into a procrastination step.

Set a specific date for when you want to accomplish something and stick to it completely. Set it around important events if you can. For example, if you are planning a vacation or will be attending a concert, make it a goal to finish a certain project or reach a specific endpoint. If you are attending a wedding, and you also need to get in shape to fit into your suit, you can make a goal to lose 10 pounds prior to the wedding.

Don't See Any Consequences

This goes along the lines of accountability, but the reason so many people don't get things done is that they do not realize the consequences until they already occur. For example, if your roof needs to be fixed, you will probably put it off because you do not see any consequences for doing so. Of course, on the night that it's pouring rain and the roof suddenly collapses, you will recognize your mistake. Start seeing the potential consequences of not getting things done. Write them down if you have to. Once you see them visually, then you are more likely to take them seriously. For example, if you need new tires on your car and you have been putting it off, then write down that you will get stranded on the freeway with four ruptured tires.

Why Getting Things Done is Critical

Here is the bottom line. The many advancements we have made in this world were done by go-getters who acted constantly. They were not done by people who refused to do the work. As you look back on history, any type of accomplishment, whether good or bad, had massive action behind it. I say bad, as well, because there have been many negative events in our history. I hope you keep your goals positive.

Getting things done creates a sense of accomplishment. No matter how much or how little you do today, it is far better than doing nothing. Nothing gets you nowhere while small steps create some progress.

Getting things done now is the ultimate productivity hack available. There are no tricks or secret formulas. It is simply a matter of doing something now, rather than nothing at all. Whatever you can manage to do within a given period of time, do it, and you will be that much closer.

Imagine having to paint a house. This is not an easy task, especially if you have a big house. Let's say, for this example, the house has 100 walls to paint. If you pain one a day, that is still something. After 100 days, which is just over three months, you will have painted the whole house. Taking three months is better than nothing at all. On certain days, when you have more time and energy, you can paint extra on those days. If painting your house is a goal, then give yourself a deadline with rewards or punishments along the way. For example, if you are not halfway done by a certain date, then cancel something you were looking forward to. Hold yourself accountable, and if you need to, have someone else hold you accountable too.

In the next chapter, I will cover many different tips to start getting things done.

Chapter 2: It's Time to Get Things Done

Now that I have covered the reason why people don't get things done; it is now time to start taking action. This chapter will be focused on various strategies to overcome the blocks in your life. Start following these, and you will be accomplishing things in no time.

Overcoming Procrastination

It's time to stop putting things off. Many of your dreams and goals have gone unfulfilled because you waited too long to start working on them. The world has also missed out on your gifts because you had the potential to create something great if you only took some action in completing it. The following are some ways to overcome one of the greatest obstacles to not getting something done: Procrastination.

Don't Catastrophize

This means that you make a bigger deal out of things than you should. This could be based on the results you might get, or the excruciating the actual task will be. In any event, you are expecting the process to be unbearable.

Here's a little tip: it won't be. We often overthink to the point that our mind creates a scenario that is not conducive to reality. The truth is, hard work, boredom, and other challenges will not kill you. You may not enjoy them on time, but you will overcome them. Also, the results we get are rarely ever at the level we imagine them to be. The thought of a fall is generally harder than the fall itself.

Always believe in yourself that you can make it through something and deal with the consequences, positive or negative, that come with it. The truth is, you can. Even if a task is as horrible as you imagined, you got through it, and it's out of the way. This is much better than thinking about it. Just get it done!

Focus on Your "Why"

You "why" is the ultimate reason for you doing something and should be used as a motivating factor for you. Many procrastinators focus on short-term gains and do not pay attention to long-term potential. This is why it's important to remember your "why." It is the end result you are expecting.

This can be used for any goal in your life, personal or professional. If you have been putting off creating a resume, then imagine yourself in your dream job. If you have been putting off organizing your room, imagine how good you will feel when you can find things easily and don't have to get around a huge mess.

Get Out Your Scheduler

Projects often do not get done because people make no time for them. They will do it when they have time, and therefore, the time will never come. You need to make time and stick to it. Get out your scheduler, whether it's an online planner, paper planner, or calendar, and start blocking off times. Whatever important tasks that need to be completed, write them down and on a specific time and date. Unless something unavoidable comes up, stick to the specific block on your schedule. When people write things down, they are holding themselves accountable. If they miss doing something, they can look at it, and it will remind them.

Be Realistic

Getting things done means you are setting yourself up for success. Do not create unrealistic goals for yourself. Set an achievable goal, and then take specific action steps to get there. For example, do not tell yourself that you will start working out five times a week in the morning immediately when you are not even a morning person. Instead, set up your workout schedule in the evening. If you ultimately want to work out in the mornings, then you can start by doing it once a week and then increasing your days. Do not expect to reach your goals instantly. Set up a long-term plan for success.

Break it Down

Tasks can often become overwhelming, and this leads to procrastination. Break them down into smaller and more manageable tasks with specific deadlines for each small task. If you are planning to landscape your home, start with a small area and give yourself the time you need in each section.

Stop With the Excuses

Here it goes: You will never be fully energized; it will never be the right time; you will often not be in the mood; conditions may never be perfect. Stop using these as excuses. Waiting for any of these will just delay you for no reason. Getting things done is not about waiting for the perfect opportunity. It is about using what you ave to create opportunity. Stop with the excuses!

Find an Accountability Partner

It can be difficult to hold yourself accountable, so find a partner to help you. Express what your goals are to this person and the deadlines that you have. Your accountability partner can then follow up with you and make sure you are staying on track. If you don't reach your deadlines, your partner's job is to grill you as to why. You guys can help each other in this manner to make it a mutual relationship.

Optimize Your Environment

Your environment will play a huge role in creating distractions. Optimize it by finding a quiet place and only having the things you absolutely need. Turn off the TV, social media (I recommend logging out so you can't access it easily), get rid of any papers or clutter that will catch your attention. How many times have you meant to start something, only to get distracted by something else? This is very common, and you must do what you can to avoid it happening to you.

Forgive Yourself

While it might be true that starting something earlier would have been more advantageous, do not beat yourself up for not doing so. You cannot change the past, so forget about it. You can make up for it though by taking advantage of the present. Learn from your past mistake of putting something off and start doing things today. If you should have gone to college five years ago, well, it's okay. You can still go now.

Procrastinators are often trying to avoid distress, but in doing so, they are ironically creating more of it. Start taking the action steps I have described above, and you will no longer be putting things off until tomorrow.

Mindfulness Meditation Technique

Many individuals are not able to get things done because they cannot live in the present moment. They are either anxious about the past or worried about the future. Both of these are unproductive thoughts to have and must be eliminated immediately. You must start focusing on the present, and mindfulness meditation techniques are a great way to do so. Bear in mind, it can take years to master the practice of meditation, so I will just go over the basics to get you started. The following are some structured meditation exercises.

Body Scan Meditation

Start by lying down on your back with your arms at your sides, palms facing up, and legs extended. Now pay close attention and observe every section of your body from head to toe. Become fully aware of any sensations or emotions you are feeling and from where they are coming from. This will bring awareness to yourself and what is happening to you. You will begin living in the present moment with real-time feelings.

Sitting Meditation

Sit in a comfortable position, preferable in a chair, with your back straight, feet flat on the floor, and your palms on your lap. Once in a comfortable position, breathe in slowly through your nose and allow it to go down to your diaphragm. Then slowly let the breath out. Focus completely on your breathing. If you get distracted by anything, note the experience and then return your attention back to your breathing.

Walking Meditation

Find a quiet space that is at least 15-20 feet in length. Walk slowly between each wall in the room and focus completely on the experience. Be aware of all of the subtle movements that are being used to keep you balanced. Do not pay attention to anything else but your walking.

Simple Mindfulness

The following are a few more mindfulness exercises. These are simple and can be practiced anywhere.

- Focus on your breathing. Take slow and deep breaths in and out. This was done in the meditative position but can also be accomplished standing up anywhere.
- Find joy in the simple pleasures of life and live in the moment.
- Accept yourself and learn to treat yourself like you would a good friend.
- Experience the environment you are in with all of your senses. Do not be in such a rush all the time. Fully taste the food you're eating, stop to smell the roses, listen to the birds chirping, and even touch some dirt. Feel your surroundings.

15 Habits of Highly Productive People

To become successful, you must mimic the habits of other successful people. The following are effective habits that productive people use every day. These individuals get things done, and you can, as well.

- Focus on the most important tasks first. These are the ones that have the most urgency, the closest deadlines, and the most with the most severe results if not done. Complete them first and then move on to other things.

- Cultivate deep work, which are your hardest, most boring, and most complicated tasks. They have to be done, and if you are not focused fully, they will be missed. Say "no" to people more often, limit distractions, set up a scheduled time for these tasks each day, and go where you do your best work, whether in the office, library, or café, etc.

- Keep a distraction list. While you are working, anytime a distraction comes up, write it down, and then get back to work. This technique works because you are giving attention to your distraction, which eases up its strength over you.

- Use the 80/20 rule. Determine the 20% of your work that requires the most attention. Look at the remaining 80% and see what you can cut out to make more time for the 20%.

- Take scheduled breaks. Even though you want to get a lot done, you cannot just work 24/7. Take scheduled breaks throughout your workday and spend the rest of the time being fully focused. For instance, spend 55 minutes working hard, then take a 10 minutes break to relax and eat something.

- Limit the number of decisions you have to make. Decisions that aren't important should not take up too much of your time or energy. For example, many productive people will wear similar outfits every day because their wardrobe is not as important as other decisions.

- Eliminate insufficient communication. Ignore and delete useless emails, do not engage in too much idle chatter, and avoid gossip, which is a complete waste of time.

- Delegate certain tasks when you can. If you are busy with your career, then you can hire people to do things like take care of your lawn or do your dry cleaning.

- Learn from your successes, as well as your mistakes. Even in success, lessons can be learned about making things more efficient.

- Plan as much as you can for things going wrong because getting caught off guard can be quite a time consumer. It is better to have a plan ahead of time than trying to come up with one urgently.

- Don't wait until you are inspired or motivated to work. Start working and get yourself inspired or motivated.

- Avoid Multitasking. Instead, focus on one task for as long as you can before moving over to the next one.

- Get enough sleep, eat well, exercise, and take time to recharge. This will give you the energy you need when it's time to be productive. Whenever you do something, put all of your effort into it, including rest.

- Take time to get better at tasks by educating yourself and improving your skills.

- Manage your time and energy. Do not waste any of them unnecessarily.

Once you start taking these action steps seriously, you will notice yourself accomplishing a lot more. I will now get into looking towards your future and the life you want to create.

Chapter 3: Visualizing a Better Future

When you learn to get things done and do them well, you will create a better future for yourself. This can become one of your motivations to get moving, as well. In this chapter, I will continue to focus on action steps to get you moving so you can get things done. Once you can visualize your future, you can create it.

How to Visualize Your Future

In this section, I will go over some ways to visualize your future so that you can create an image that inspires you. This is a powerful tool that helps you create the future you want. Will it turn out exactly as you see it? Definitely not. There are too many variables that factor in. However, always keeping that picture in mind means that you will push yourself harder to achieve the success you want. As you see your reality a few years down the line, you will expect more out of yourself. Start by answering the following questions. Remember, these are the answers you hope to give five, 10, 15, or whatever years down the line.

- When someone asks you what you do for work, what do you tell them?
- Describe all of your surroundings in great detail, including your house, the city, neighborhood, and what's nearby. Where do you spend most of your free time?
- What is the atmosphere like at work and in your home, and how do you contribute to it?
- What is your greatest accomplishment? What brings you the most pride?

- Are there any regrets that you have?

- What are the specific steps you took to get where you are?

- What advice would you give to someone else who wants to be where you are?

- What problems arose along the way?

After answering these questions, you will understand where you want to be and have an idea of how to get there.

More Tips for Visualization

Once you begin visualizing your future, then you have it ingrained in your mind. It becomes much harder to let it go. Of course, this does not mean that it's a guarantee. You still must put in the work and make the right moves. For example, if you want to start a business, you can picture the type, how big it will be, where it should be located, how it will look, and whether you plan to have employees or not, among other things. Seeing is believing, though, and the following tips will help you start believing in yourself and your future.

Visualize Your New Life

One way to become excited about your goals is to imagine what your life will be like when you achieve them. For example, if you plan on increasing your salary, imagine that extra money coming in. How much will it be, and what will you be able to do with it? What will you be doing to get that extra money, whether it's through work, investing, or starting a business, etc.? Anything you can imagine about what your life will be like, try to picture it in your mind.

Create a Vision Board

Start collecting images, quotes, articles, and any other visual representations that you feel reflect your future. For instance, you can collect a specific item from a state if you plan on living there someday. This will help you trigger inspiration and hold you accountable for your dreams.

Write Down Your goals

This is a common practice and is touted as being very effective by most productive people. If you are not fond of vision boards, you can write down your goals in lieu of that practice. You may also do it in conjunction with each other for added benefits.

Let Yourself Zone Out

If you find yourself daydreaming at certain times, let it happen. Your mind is trying to tell you something about what you want. Many geniuses in the past, including Einstein, would zone out throughout the day. During these moments, a bolt of inspiration can strike, and great plans can be made. Of course, you cannot daydream all the time, or nothing will get done, which defeats the purpose.

However, when you can, take the time to do it.

Say Your Goals Out Loud

Whatever you have planned, whether short-term or long-term, say it out loud, so the universe knows. This also triggers your brain to understand what you want, so it also starts thinking towards that direction.

Think About What You Want and not What You Don't Want

There is a phenomenon known as the Law of Attraction. According to the rules, what you focus on is what the universe delivers to you, even if you're thinking about it in a negative way. So, even if you're thinking about poverty in terms of not falling into it, you will still attract it because it is in your mind. Therefore, it is better not to even visualize poverty but just think about becoming wealthy.

Life When You Get Things Done

All the information and strategies I have gone over in this book lead up to one thing: Getting things done. That is how you achieve what you want in life. You simply must take action and go for what you want. The action steps in the previous chapters provide a way to make goal-getting easier by providing direction, focus, and motivation. I will end this book by over the many benefits of getting things. Getting things done, or GTD is an actual process and state of mind. When you start incorporating it, you will notice many changes during and after.

A Feeling of Relaxed Control

You will feel in control of your life because you are taking active steps to create it. This may be the number one benefit of getting things done. Performing frequent assessments, processing information, and acting on it can make your mind feel like it's water, where it just flows and makes decisions naturally. It takes time for everyone to get to this state.

Your Thinking Will Be Stimulated

When you get things done, your thinking will be stimulated in advance. You will continuously be thinking about the little and big projects in your life, and they will rarely if ever, slip by you. Procrastination will be an afterthought, and you will always be ahead of the curve.

More Organization and Less Clutter

Getting things done means you will clean off your desk literally and figuratively. You will accomplish your tasks and keep your work area organized too. When you get things done, you will be more versatile, and it will become easier to make and keep commitments. In addition, you will be able to keep others accountable for their commitments.

Thinking is good, but overthinking can be detrimental. It can lead to worry, anxiety, and fear. One of the best ways to avoid this is by acting. Worrying occurs when you have a moment for it. When you act, you are doing and have less time to worry.

The entire point of getting things done is just that, getting things done. This is how you accomplish your goals and start living the life you imagine. There are so many get-rich-quick schemes and people promising others the world if they just do a few simple things. With this book, I wanted to provide many different action steps for you so you can tidy up, clear out unnecessary garbage, both emotional and physical, and start working on your dreams. It may take time, but if you're moving in the right direction, that is what matters most.

PART V

Chapter 1: Self-Care Is the Best Care

"It is so important to take time for yourself and find clarity. The most important relationship is the one you have with yourself."

-Diane Von Furstenberg

Self-care is any activity that we deliberately do to improve our own well-being, whether it is physical, emotional, mental, or spiritual. The importance of taking care of one's self cannot be denied, as even health care training focuses on making sure healthcare workers are caring for themselves. If you do not take care of yourself, eventually, every other aspect o your life will fall apart, including your ability to help others.

This is a very simple concept, yet it is highly overlooked in the grand scheme of things. People lack the tendency to look after themselves and put their needs before anyone else. Good self-care is essential to improving our mood and reducing our anxiety levels. It will do wonders for reducing exhaustion and burnout, which is very common in our fast-paced world. It will also lead to positive improvements in our relationships.

One thing to note is that self-care does not mean forcing ourselves to do something we don't like, no matter how enjoyable it is to other people. For example, if your friends are forcing you to go to a party you rather not attend, then giving in is not taking care of yourself. If you would rather stay in and watch a movie, then that's what you should do, and it will be better for your well-being.

How Does Self-Care Work

It is difficult to pinpoint exactly what self-care is, as it is personal for everybody. Some people love to pamper themselves by going to the spa, while others enjoy physical activities like hiking, biking, or swimming. Some individuals take up art or other hobbies, like writing or playing a musical instrument. These activities are all different but will have the same type of benefits for the individuals engaging in them.

The main factor to consider when engaging in self-care is to determine if you enjoy the activity in question. If not, then it's time to move on. Self-care is an active choice that you actually have to plan out. It is time you set aside for yourself to make sure all of your needs are met. If you use a planner of any sort, make sure to dedicate some space for your particular self-care activities. Also, let people who need to know about your plans so you can become more committed. Pay special attention to how you feel afterward. The objective of any self-care activity is to make yourself feel better. If this is not happening, then it's time to change the activity.

While self-care, as a whole, is individualized, there is a basic checklist to consider.

- Create a list of things you absolutely don't want to do during the self-care process. For instance, not checking emails, not answering the phone, avoiding activities you don't enjoy, or not going to specific gatherings, like a house party.

- Eat nutritious and healthy meals most of the time, while indulging once in a while.
- Get the proper amount of sleep according to your needs.
- Avoid too many negative things, like news or social media.
- Exercise regularly.
- Spend appropriate time with your loved ones. These are the people you genuinely enjoy and not forced relationships.
- Look for opportunities to enjoy yourself and laugh.
- Do at least one relaxing activity a day, like taking a bath, going for a walk, or cooking a meal.

Self-care is extremely important and should not be an anomaly in your life.

How Does Self-Care Improve Self-Esteem and Self-Confidence?

To bring everything full circle, self-care plays a major role in improving self-esteem and self-confidence. It is easy to see how taking care of yourself will also make you feel better about yourself overall. All of these are actually inter-related, and a lack of one showcases a lack of the other. While caring for yourself also improves your self-esteem and self-confidence, not having self-esteem or self-confidence also leads to a lack of self-care. Basically, you believe that you are not good enough to be taken care of.

People with high self-esteem and self-confidence value themselves as much as they value others, and have no issues with making sure they're taken care of. They realize that it does not make them selfish or inconsiderate to think in this manner. Even if other people try to make them feel that way, a self-confident person will just brush off the criticism. An important thing to note is that when you take care of yourself, it does not mean you don't care about other people. It simply means you have enough self-love to not place yourself on the backburner.

Many people work so hard to try and please everyone else. This is one of the telltale signs of low self-esteem. While they're busy worried about other peoples' needs, their own get neglected, which will wear them down over time. The more they're unable to please someone, the harder they will try. What people in this situation don't realize is that some people are impossible to please, and it is not their responsibility to please them. That is up to the individual.

Poor self-care will eventually lead to poor self-image. It is possible that a person already has this initially. Self-care includes taking care of your hygienic and grooming needs. If you don't take the time to make yourself look good, this will significantly impact the value you place on yourself. When you are t work, among your friends, or just walking around town, not feeling like you look good will ultimately make you feel like you don't belong anywhere. Your confidence levels will plummet due to this.

Your health is another aspect to consider. Poor self-care means bad sleeping habits, unhealthy diets, lack of exercise, and more self-destructive behaviors. Your poor health practices can result in chronic illnesses down the line, like heart disease or diabetes. Once again, diminished health will lead to reduced self-confidence and self-esteem. Ask yourself now if putting other people ahead of you is worth it? I've got some news for you. The people who demand the most from you are probably looking out for themselves first.

The less a person takes care of themselves, the more their self-esteem and self-confidence will decline. It turns into a vicious downward cycle. This is why it is important to focus on all of these areas equally. When you find yourself neglecting your own self-care practices, it is time to shift your direction and bring your attention back to your needs. Ignoring your needs will ultimately lead to your fall. We will discuss specific practices and techniques for improving self-care in the next chapter.

Chapter 2:

What Does Good Self-Care Look Like?

Good Self-Care Practices

The following are some ways that good self-care will look like. If you find yourself having these qualities, then you are on the right path.

Taking Responsibility for Your Happiness

When you engage in self-care, it is truly self-care. This means you only rely on yourself, and nobody else, to make sure your needs are met. You realize that your happiness is no one else's responsibility but your own. You alone have the ability to control your outcomes. As a result of this independence, you will develop the skills and attitude you need to care for your own physical, mental, emotional, and spiritual well-being.

You Become Assertive With Others

People often take assertiveness for rudeness. This is not true, but if people believe that standing firm for what you want is rude, then that's their problem. Once you reach a certain mindset where self-care is important to you, then you will be unapologetically assertive. This means you have the ability to say "no" with confidence and stand by it. "No" is a complete sentence, and people will realize that quickly when they hear it from you.

You Treat Yourself As You Would a Close Friend

It's interesting how we believe that other people deserve better treatment from us than we do ourselves. We have a tendency to put our best friends in front of us, no matter how detrimental it is to our lives. This behavior stops once we engage in proper self-care. At this point, you will treat yourself as good as, or even better, than you treat your most beloved friends.

You Are Not Afraid to Ask for What You Want

Once you learn to take care of yourself, you also see your value increase within your mind. This means having an understanding that your voice, opinion, and needs matter, just like anybody with high self-esteem and self-confidence, would. As a result, you will not be afraid to ask for what you want, even if you might not get it.

Your Life Is Set Around Your Own Values

Once you practice self-care, you learn to check in with yourself before making important decisions. You always make sure the choices you are about to make line up with your purpose and values. If they go against them, then it's not a path you choose. This goes for the career you choose, where you decide to live, and the relationships you maintain in your life.

While all of the traits are focused on self, but it will lead to better relationships with other people too. When you practice self-care, you are in a better state in every aspect of your being. This gives you the ability to take care of and help those you need you, as well. Self-care is not an option, but a necessity, and it must never be ignored. Taking care of yourself is not selfish, no matter what anybody tells you. If someone tries to make you feel guilty over this matter, then consider distancing or removing them from your life. You are not obligated to maintain relationships with people.

Chapter 3: Demanding Your Own Self-Care

We went over the importance of self-care, and now we will focus on making it a reality in your life. If you want self-care to occur, you must be willing to demand it. The world is full of people who expect you to be at there beck-and-call every moment of the day. Some of these individuals are those who are closest to us, like friends or family members. This can make it harder to make our demands heard, but there is no way around it. Taking care of yourself is not an idea you can budge on. It is extremely important. We will go over several ways to maintain your ability for self-care in your life and provide detailed action steps to help you progress in this area.

Setting Healthy Boundaries

One of the biggest obstacles to self-care is other people who surround you. These are the true selfish individuals, whether they realize it or not, who believe they can barge in on your life and deserve all of your attention. They will take advantage of you, and if you are not careful, they will completely gain control of your emotions, and even your life. For proper self-care to occur, you must set firm and healthy boundaries with people. The following are steps that need to become mainstays in your life.

Identify and Name Your Limits

You must understand what your emotional, physical, mental, and spiritual limits are. If you do not know, then you will never be able to set real boundaries with people. Determine what behaviors you can tolerate and accept, and then consider what makes you feel uncomfortable. Identifying and separating these traits will help us determine our lines.

Stay Tuned Into Your Feelings

Two major emotions that are red flags that indicate a person is crossing a barrier are resentment or discomfort. Whenever you are having these feelings, it is important to determine why. Resentment generally comes from people taking advantage of us or feelings of being unappreciated. In this instance, we are likely pushing ourselves beyond our limits because we feel guilty. Guilt-trips is a weapon that many people use to get their way. It is important to recognize when someone is trying to make you feel guilty because they are way overstepping their boundaries. Resentment could also be due to someone imposing their own views or values onto us. When someone makes you feel uncomfortable, that is another indication of a boundary crossed. Stay in tune with both of these emotions.

Don't Be Afraid of Being Direct

With some people, setting boundaries is easy because they have a similar communication style. They can simply read your cues and back off when needed. For other individuals, a more direct approach is needed. Some people just don't get the hint that they've crossed a line. You must communicate to them in a firm way that they have crossed your limits, and you need some space. A respectful person will honor your wishes without hesitation. If they don't, then that's on them. Your personal space is more important than their feelings.

Give Yourself Permission to Set Boundaries

The potential downfalls to personal limits are fear, self-doubt, and guilt. We may fear the other person's response when we set strong boundaries. Also, we may feel guilty if they become emotional about it. We may even have self-doubt on whether we can maintain these limits in the long run. Many individuals have the mindset that in order to be a good daughter, son, parent, or friend, etc., we have to say "yes" all the time. They often wonder if they deserve to have boundaries and limits with those closest to them. The answer is, yes, you do. You need to give yourself permission to set limits with people because they are essential to maintaining healthy relationships too. Boundaries are also a sign of self-respect. Never feel bad for respecting yourself.

Consider Your Past and Present

Determine what roles you have played throughout your life in the various relationships you have had. Were you the one who was always the caretaker? If so, then your natural tendency may be to put others before yourself. Also, think about your relationships now. Are you the one always taking care of things, or is it a reciprocal relationship? For example, are you always the one making plans, buying gifts, having dinner parties, and being responsible for all of the important aspects of the relationships? If this is the case, then tuning into your needs is especially important here. If you are okay with the dynamics of the relationship, then that's fine. I can't tell you how to feel. However, if you feel anger and resentment over this, then it's time to let your feeling be known, unapologetically.

Be Assertive

Once again, this does not mean being rude, even though some people will interpret it that way. Being assertive simply means being firm, which is important when reminding someone about your boundaries. Creating boundaries alone is not enough. You also have to stand by them and let people know immediately if they've crossed them. Let the person know in a respectful but strong tone that you are uncomfortable with where they're going, and they need to give you some space. Assertive communication is a necessity.

Start Small

Setting boundaries is a skill that takes a while to develop, especially if it's something you've never done before. Therefore, start with a small boundary, like no phone calls after a certain time at night. Make sure to follow through;

otherwise, the boundary is worthless. From here, make larger boundaries based on your comfort level.

Eliminating Toxicity and Not Caring About Losing Friends

If you plan on making self-care a priority in your life, I think that's great, and so should you. However, some people will have a problem with this. People don't always like it when their friends, family members, or acquaintances, etc., put themselves at the forefront of their lives. Once again, that is their problem, not yours. What is your problem, though, is distancing or even eliminating these individuals from your life. We will go over that in this section because part of self-care is eliminating toxicity from your life and not feeling bad about it.

Don't Expect People to Change

While everyone deserves a chance to redeem themselves, there comes the point where we must accept that people cannot change by force. They have to find it within themselves to make this change, and it is not our responsibility to do so. You may yearn to be the one who changes them, but it's usually a hopeless project. Toxic individuals are motivated by their problems. They use them to get the attention they need. Stop being the one to give it to them.

Establish and Maintain Boundaries

I already went in-depth on this, so I won't revisit it too much here. Just know that toxic people will push you to work harder and harder for them, while you completely ignore your own needs. This is exhausting and unacceptable. Create the boundaries you need with these individuals based on your own limits.

Don't Keep Falling for Crisis Situations

Toxic people will make you feel like they need you always because they are constantly in a crisis situation of some sort. It is a neverending cycle. When a person is in a perpetual crisis, it is of their own doing. They often create drama purposely to get extra attention. You may feel guilty for ignoring them, but remember that their being manipulative and not totally genuine.

I am not saying that you can't ever help someone who is going through a hard time. Of course, you can. Just don't start believing that you're responsible for their success or failure.

Focus on the Solution

Toxic individuals will give you a lot to be angry and sad about. If you focus on this, then you will just become miserable. You must focus on the solution, which, in this case, is removing drama and toxicity from your life. Recognize the fact that you will have less emotional stress once you remove this person from your life. If you let them, they will suck away all of your energy.

Accept Your Own Difficulties and Weaknesses

A toxic person will know how to exploit your weaknesses and use them against you. For example, if you are easy to guilt-trip, they will have you feel guilty every time you pull away from them. If you get to know yourself better and recognize these weaknesses, then you can better manage them and protect yourself. This goes along with creating self-awareness, which we discussed in chapter two. When you accept your weaknesses, you can work on fixing them and balance them with your strengths.

They Won't Go Easily

Recognize that a toxic individual may resist being removed from your life. Actually, if they don't resist, I will be pleasantly surprised. They may throw tantrums, but this is because they can't control or manipulate you anymore. They will even increase their previous tactics with more intensity. It is a trap, and you must not fall for it. Stay firm in your desire to leave and keep pushing forward. If they suck you back in, good luck trying to get out again.

Choose Your Battles Carefully

Fighting with a toxic person is exhausting and usually not worth it. You do not need to engage in every battle with them. They are just trying to instigate you.

Surround Yourself With Healthy relationships

Once you have removed a toxic person, or persons, from your life, then avoid falling into the trap with someone else. Fill your circle with happy and healthy relationships, so there is no room for any toxicity. Always remember the signs of a toxic person, so you can avoid them wholeheartedly in the future.

How to Focus on Self-Care

Now that we have worked to set boundaries and eliminate toxic people from our lives, it is time to focus on ourselves and the self-care we provide. The following are some self-care tips, according to psychologist, Dr. Tchiki Davis, Ph.D.

Pay Attention to Your Sleep

Sleep is an essential part of taking care of yourself. You must make it part of your routine because it will play a huge role in your emotional and physical well-being. There are many things that can wreak havoc on your sleep patterns, like stress, poor diet, watching television, or looking at your phone as you're trying to fall asleep. Think about your night routine. Are you eating right before bed or taking in a lot of sugar and caffeine? Are you working nonstop right up until bedtime? Have you given yourself some time to wind down before going to sleep? All of these factors are important to consider, as they will affect your sleep patterns. If you can, put away any phones, tablets, and turn off the television at least 30 minutes before you plan on going to bed.

Take Care of Your Gut

We often neglect our digestive tract, but it plays a major role in our health and overall well-being. When our gut is not working well, it makes us feel sluggish, bloated, and nonproductive. Pay attention to the food you eat as it will determine the health of your gut. It is best to avoid food with excess salt, sugar, cholesterol, or unhealthy fats. Stick to foods that are high in fiber, protein, healthy fats, and complex carbs. Some good options are whole grains, nuts, lean meats, fruits and vegetables, beans, and fish.

Exercise and Physical Activity Is Essential

Regular exercise is great for both physical and mental health. The physical benefits are obvious. However, many people do not realize that exercise will help the body release certain hormones like endorphins and serotonin. These are often called feel-good hormones because they play a major role in affecting our mood in a positive way. The release of these hormones will give us energy too, which will make us want to exercise more. Once exercise becomes a habit, it will be hard to break. Decide for yourself what your exercise routine will be, whether it's going to the gym, walking around the neighborhood, or playing a game of tennis.

Consider a Mediterranean Diet

While this is not a dietary book, the Mediterranean diet is considered the healthiest diet in the world because of its extreme health benefits. The food groups and ingredients that are used will increase energy, brain function, and has amazing benefits like heart and digestive tract health. The food also does not lack flavor, which shatters the myth that healthy food does not taste good.

Take a Self-Care Trip

Even if you are not much of a traveler, getting away once in a while can do wonders for your mental health. So often, our environment will make us feel stressed out, and it's good to remove ourselves from it for a couple of days. You do not have to take a trip abroad here. Of course, that is certainly an option. A simple weekend trip is perfectly fine. Just get yourself out of your normal routine and be by yourself for a while.

Get Outside

Nature and sunlight can be great medicines. It can help you reduce stress or worry, and has many great health benefits. Doing some physical activity outside, like hiking or gardening, are also great options.

Bring a Pet Into Your Life

Pets can bring you a lot of joy, and the responsibility they come with can boost your self-confidence by having to care for another living creature. Dogs are especially great at helping to reduce stress and anxiety. Animal therapy has been used to help people suffering from disorders lie PTSD, as well.

Get Yourself Organized

Organizing your life and doing some decluttering can do wonders for your mental and emotional health. Decide what area of your life needs to be organized. Do you need to clear your desk, clean out the fridge, or declutter your closet? Do you need to get a calendar or planner and schedule your life better? Whatever you can do to get yourself more organized, do it. Being organized allows you to know how to take better care of yourself.

Cook Yourself Meals At Home

People often neglect the benefits of a good home-cooked meal. They opt, instead, for fast-food or microwave dinners. These types of meals will make you full but will lack in essential nutrients that your body needs. Cooking nutritious meals at home will allow you to use the correct ingredients, so you can feel full and satisfied. Cooking alone can also be great therapy for people.

Read Regularly

Self-help books are a great read. However, do not limit yourself to these. You can also read books on subjects that you find fascinating or books that simply provide entertainment.

Schedule Your Self-Care Time

Just like you would write down an appointment time in your planner, also block out specific times for self-care activities. Stick to this schedule religiously, unless a true emergency comes up. This means that if a friend calls you to go out, you should respectfully decline their request and focus on yourself.

Chapter 4: How to Be Happy Being Alone

The final section of this book will focus on being alone and how to be happy about it. When you start engaging in self-care, you will also be spending much more time by yourself. A lot of people have a hard time dealing with this concept, especially if they're used to being around people all the time. However, for proper self-care, you have to be okay with being alone once in a while.

Accept Some Alone Time

The following are some tips to help you become happy with being alone. Soon, you will realize that your own company is the best kind.

Do Not Compare Yourself to Others

We are referring to your social life here. Do not compare to others, and do not feel like you must live as others do. If you do this, you may become jealous of a person's social circle or lifestyle. It is better to focus on yourself and what makes you happy. If you plan on spending significant time alone, then you cannot pay attention to what other people are doing.

Step Away From Social Media

If strolling through your social media page makes you feel left out, then take a step back and put it away for a while. During self-care moments, you are the focus, not what is happening with others online. Also, what people post on their pages is not always true. Many individuals have been known to exaggerate, or even flat-out lie on social media platforms. You may be feeling jealous or left out for no reason. Try banning yourself from social media for 24-48 hours, and see how it makes you feel.

Take a Break From Your Phone

Avoid making or receiving calls. Let the important people in your life know that you will be away from your phone for a while, so they don't worry. When you are alone, really try to be alone.

Allow Time for Your Mind to Wander

If you feel unusual about doing nothing, it is probably because you have not allowed yourself to be in this position for a while. Carve out a small amount of time where you stay away from TV, music, the internet, and even books. Use this time to just sit quietly with your thoughts. Find a comfortable spot to sit or lie down, then just let your mind wander and see where it takes you. This may seem strange the first time, but with practice, you will get used to the new freedom.

Take Yourself on a Date

You don't need to be with someone else to enjoy a night out on the town. Take a self-date and enjoy your own company for a while. Go to a movie by yourself, stop by a nice restaurant, or just go do an activity you enjoy. If you are not used to hanging out alone, give it some time and you will become more comfortable with it. Take yourself on that solo date.

Exercise

We have mentioned exercise and physical activity a lot, but that's because it has so many great benefits related to self-care. Exercising will uplift your mood, and make it more enjoyable to be by yourself. Those feel-good hormones will provide a lot of benefits during these times.

Take Advantage of the Perks of Being Alone

Some people have spent so much time with other people that they've forgotten the perks of being alone. There are many to consider. First of all, you do not have to ask anyone's permission to do anything; you will have more personal space, can enjoy the activities you want to do, and don't have to worry about upsetting anyone. If you want, you can even have a solo dance party in your living room, Tom Cruise style. There are many advantages to being alone, so use them.

Find a Creative Outlet

It is beneficial to use some of your alone time to work on something creative. This can be painting, sculpting, music, writing, or any other creative endeavors. In fact, you can get out the watercolors and start fingerpainting. Creativity will bring a lot of joy into your life. It will make you happier about being alone.

Take Time to Self-Reflect

Being alone will give you the opportunity to self-reflect on your life. You won't care so much about being alone when you are coming up with important answers to your life.

Make Plans for Your Future

Planning out your life for five or ten years down the line will give you something important to do, and something to look forward to. Alone time is the perfect opportunity to determine these plans.

Make Plans for Solo Outings

Plan your solo outings based on what you like to do, whether it's a farmer's market, hiking, riding your bike, or going camping alone. Mak plans that will excite you, and you will be taking care of yourself while also being okay alone.

There are numerous topics that we went over in this chapter, but they all relate back to one theme: Self-care. Always remember that to take proper care of yourself, you must consider the following ideas:

- Setting Boundaries

- Avoiding and ridding yourself of toxic people

- Focus on yourself and your needs

- Be okay with being alone

Focus on these areas, and you will be demanding your own self-care without ever apologizing for it.

CPSIA information can be obtained
at www.ICGtesting.com
Printed in the USA
BVHW060949100920
588544BV00012B/1495